THE STORY OF GLASS

This edition published 2025
by Living Book Press
Copyright © Living Book Press, 2025

ISBN: 978-1-76153-455-3 (hardcover)
         978-1-76153-466-9 (softcover)

First published in 1916.

This edition is based on the The Penn Publishing Company printing by 1916.

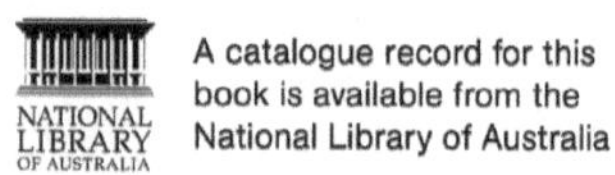

THE STORY OF GLASS

by

SARA WARE BASSETT

Contents

To G. C.

*a patient listener and a helpful critic I inscribe
this book as a reminder of many happy hours
which we spent together in the Old World
S. W. B.*

CHAPTER I

A FRIENDLY FEUD

EAN CABOT "lived around." She did not live around because nobody wanted her, however; on the contrary, she lived around because so many people wanted her. Both her father and mother had died when Jean was a baby and so until she was twelve years old she had been brought up by a cousin of her mother's. Then the cousin had married a missionary and had gone to teach the children in China, and China, as you will agree, was no place for an American girl to go to school. Therefore Jean was sent to Boston and put in charge of her uncle, Mr. Robert Cabot. Uncle Bob was delighted with the arrangement, for they were great friends, Jean and this boy-uncle of hers.

But no sooner did she arrive in Boston and settle down to live on Beacon Hill than up rose Uncle Tom Curtis, Jean's other uncle, who lived in Pittsburgh. He made a dreadful fuss because Jean had gone to Uncle Bob's to live. *He* wanted her out in Pittsburgh, and he wrote that Fräulein Decker, who

1

was his housekeeper, and had been governess to Jean's own mother, wanted her too.

That started Hannah, Uncle Bob's housekeeper.

"The very idea," she said, "of that German woman thinking they want Jean in Pittsburgh as much as we want her here in Boston. Didn't I bring up Jean's father, I'd like to know; and her Uncle Bob as well? I guess I can be trusted to bring up another Cabot. It's ridiculous—that's what it is—perfectly *ree*-diculous!" That was Hannah's favorite expression—"Ree-diculous!" "I'd like my job," went on Hannah, "sending that precious child to Pittsburgh where her white dresses would get all grimed up with coal soot."

But Hannah's scorn of Pittsburgh did not settle the matter.

Instead Mr. Carleton, Uncle Tom Curtis's lawyer, came to Boston as fast as he could get there and one afternoon presented himself at Uncle Bob's house on Beacon Hill. Uncle Bob was in the library when he arrived and the two men sat down before the fire, for it was a chilly day in early spring. After they had said a few pleasant things about the weather, and Uncle Bob had inquired for Uncle Tom, they really got started on what they wanted to say and my—how they did talk! It was all good-natured talk, for Uncle Bob liked Uncle Tom Curtis very much; nevertheless Uncle Bob and Uncle Tom's lawyer did talk pretty hard and pretty fast, for they had lots of things to say.

At last Uncle Bob Cabot rose from his leather chair and going to the fireplace gave the blazing logs a vicious little poke.

He was becoming nettled. Anybody could see that.

"The Curtises have not a whit more title to the child than I have," he burst out. "You are a lawyer, Carleton, and you know that. I am just as much Jean's uncle as Tom Curtis is; in fact I think I am more her uncle because I am her father's own brother. I'm a Cabot, and so is Jean. I should think that ought to be enough. Who would she live with, if not with the Cabots?"

Mr. Carleton cleared his throat.

"You certainly have a strong claim to the little girl," he agreed. "But you see my other client puts up an equally convincing story. In fact, he uses almost your identical words. He says he is Jean's mother's own brother, and argues no one can have a closer right than that."

"But what does he know about bringing up a little girl? Isn't he an old bachelor?"

"You are not married yourself, Mr. Cabot."

"Well, no. So I'm not. However, that's neither here nor there. Tom Curtis is fifty if he's a day. He is too old to bring up a child, Carleton."

"He complains that you are only thirty, and too young."

Mr. Robert Cabot, who was walking excitedly about the room, turned quickly.

"But I have Hannah. You do not know Hannah or you would feel differently. It is hard to tell you what Hannah is. You just have to know her. She is the mainspring of my household. Not only does she cook, clean, mend, and market for me; she does a score of things besides. Why, I couldn't live without her. She is one of those motherly souls whose wisdom is of the sages. She has been in our family since I was a baby. Most of my bringing up, in fact, was due to her and," he added whimsically, "behold the work of her hands!"

Mr. Carleton smiled.

"I cannot deny the product is good, Mr. Cabot. But again, all these arguments you put forth Mr. Tom Curtis also reechoes in behalf of his German Fräulein. She too has been for years in the Curtis family and brought up their children, and Mr. Curtis feels that since she trained Jean's mother she is eminently the person to train Jean."

"Humph!"

"The claims seem about equal."

"No, they're not. That's where you are wrong. Allowing everything else to be equal even you must grant that there is one serious objection of which you have not spoken. Mr. Tom Curtis lives in *Pittsburgh!* That is enough to overthrow the whole thing. Pittsburgh! Think of bringing up a child in Pittsburgh when she could be brought up in Boston. Boston, my good man, is intellectually—well, of course I do not wish to appear prejudiced, but you will, I am sure, admit that Boston——"

Mr. Bob Cabot dropped helplessly into his chair, leaving the sentence unfinished. There seemed to be no words in the English language adequate to express what, in Mr. Bob Cabot's estimation, Boston actually was.

Mr. Carleton started to laugh, but after glancing furtively at Mr. Bob Cabot he changed his mind and coughed instead.

"We all grant Boston is without an intellectual peer," he answered with a grave inclination of his head. "Even I, who was born in Indiana, grant that, although out in my state we think we run you a close second. Boston moreover has a background of which we in the West cannot boast—history, you know, and all that sort of thing. It would be a great privilege for little Miss Jean Cabot to receive a home and an education in Boston. There are, however, many fine things in Pittsburgh; it is not all soot, or panting factories."

"I suppose not. Jean's mother was a Pittsburgh girl, and certainly she was a wonderful type of woman. Yet you cannot tell what result a Boston environment might have had on such a nature as hers. She might have been even nearer perfection. Yet after all she was quite fine enough for human clay, Carleton, quite fine enough. And the little girl promises to be like her—an uncommonly sweet, gentle child, and pretty, too—very pretty. To send her to Pittsburgh—hang it all! Why must Tom Curtis live in Pittsburgh?"

"Mr. Curtis, as you seem to have forgotten, Mr. Cabot, is the owner of one of the largest plate glass factories in the country. He has built up a fortune by his business and he is no more ready to hurl his life's work to the winds and come to Boston to live than you are to toss aside your own business and move to Pittsburgh. And by the way, speaking of business, Mr. Cabot, if it does not seem an impertinent question, what is *your* business?"

"My business? Well, for a good many years my chief business seemed to be getting over a bad knee I got when playing tackle on the Harvard football eleven. We wiped up the ground with Yale, though, so it was worth it. Of late I spend more or less time in seeing that Hannah does not feed me too well and starve herself. Part of my business, too, is to argue with disagreeable old lawyers like yourself, Carleton." Mr. Bob Cabot chuckled. "When I am not doing some of these things and have the surplus time I am incidentally an interior decorator. Oh, I do not go out papering and painting; oh dear, no! I just tell other people how to spend a fortune furnishing their houses. I advise brocade hangings, Italian marbles and every sort of rare and beautiful thing, and since I do not have these luxuries to pay for I find my vocation a tremendously interesting one."

"You have set a worthy example in your own house," observed Mr. Carleton, glancing about with admiration.

"Oh, I've done a little—not much. I like the old landscape paper in this library; some of my antique furniture, too, is rather nice. I picked up many of the best pieces in the South. The house itself came to me from my father, and I have altered it very little, as I was anxious to keep its old colonial atmosphere. Hannah and I live here most peacefully with a waitress and inside man to help us. With Jean added to the household we shall have just the touch of young life that we need. I am very fond of children, and——"

"You seem very certain that Jean is to settle with you, Mr. Cabot. Now let me own up to something; although Mr. Tom Curtis sent me to have this talk with you and pave the way, it chances—no, chance is not the right word—on the contrary it is an intentional fact that Mr. Tom Curtis is at this very moment here in Boston."

Mr. Bob Cabot started.

"Tom Curtis here!"

"Yes. He is putting up at the University Club, and he wanted me to ask you if you would be so good as to dine there with him to-night."

"So he has come over to enter the fray himself, has he? Well, well! Why didn't he come right here? Of course I'll join him. I always liked Tom Curtis. The only things I have against him are that he *will* live in Pittsburgh—and that he wants Jean."

Mr. Carleton rose with satisfaction. At least part of his mission had been successfully accomplished. He could afford to overlook the slur on Pittsburgh which, as it happened, was his home as well as that of Mr. Tom Curtis.

"Then I'll call up Mr. Curtis," he said, "and tell him he may expect you. Will seven o'clock be all right?"

"Certainly. I suppose I shall not see you again, Carleton?"

Mr. Carleton hesitated.

"It is just possible that I may drop in on you and Mr. Curtis after dinner."

"Oh, I see. A plot."

"Not at all. I have some business to settle with Mr. Curtis before I return to Pittsburgh."

"Going back to that grimy coal hole, are you?" blustered Mr. Bob Cabot. "How you fellows can live there when you might spend your days in Bost——"

The door slammed.

Mr. Carleton was gone.

Shrugging his shoulders Mr. Bob Cabot glanced at the clock. He had just about time to dash off a necessary letter, dress, and get to the University Club.

"Hannah!" he called.

A small dark-haired woman appeared in the doorway. She had sharp little black eyes that twinkled a great deal, and she had a mouth that turned up at the corners; furthermore she had a plump figure neatly dressed in gray, and a white apron tied behind in an enormous and very spirited bow.

"Yes, Mr. Bob."

"Hannah, Mr. Tom Curtis is in town with a rascal of a lawyer. They have come to see about taking Jean to live in Pittsburgh."

"Pittsburgh! My soul, Mr. Bob! You'll not let her go, of course. Pittsburgh, indeed! Don't we know that Boston——"

"We certainly do, Hannah. Nobody knows what Boston is better than we do. But Mr. Tom Curtis unfortunately was not born in Boston."

"More's the pity! Still, I suppose he cannot be blamed for that. It wasn't really his fault."

Mr. Bob Cabot laughed and dropped a big, kindly hand on the shoulder of the woman beside him.

"I will try and impress upon him all that he has missed when I see him to-night. I am to dine with him at the University Club at seven."

"You're not dining out!" ejaculated Hannah in dismay.

"I'm afraid so."

"Oh, Mr. Bob! And fried chicken for dinner—just the way you like it, too."

"I'm sorry, Hannah."

"And me browning all those sweet potatoes!"

"I'm lots more disappointed than you are—truly I am. It can't be helped, though. Now let me finish this letter and you go and lay out my dress shirt and studs and things, or I'll be late."

Hannah darted from the room.

"I made you a Brown Betty pudding, too, Mr. Bob!" she called over her shoulder. "But no matter. There is no evil without some good; your trousers are freshly pressed and handsome as pictures—if I do say it as shouldn't. I'll lay 'em out for you, and your dinner coat as well. But to think of that pudding! Why couldn't Mr. Curtis have invited you the night the beef stew was scorched."

Promptly on the stroke of seven Uncle Bob Cabot presented himself at the University Club, where Uncle Tom Curtis was waiting for him, and the two men grasped hands cordially. How big Uncle Tom Curtis looked and, despite Hannah's remarks, how rosy and how clean! And what a nice smile he had! The dinner was extraordinarily good. The filet was done to a turn, and there was just enough seasoning on the mushrooms. As for the grilled potatoes, even Hannah herself couldn't have improved upon them. An old Harvard "grad" came over from the next table and greeted Uncle Tom Curtis, telling him he did not look a day older than when he was in college, and in spite of his gray hairs Uncle Tom Curtis seemed to believe it. Then they talked of the last Harvard boat race; the winning eleven; the D. K. E. with its initiation pranks; and the old professors. And after the other man had left the waiter brought coffee which was deliciously hot and cheese that was exactly ripe enough. Uncle Tom Curtis seemed to have no end of stories at which Uncle Bob Cabot laughed until he was very red in the face, and afterward Uncle Bob told some stories and Uncle Tom Curtis sat back in his chair and laughed and wiped his eyes and mopped his forehead. Then Uncle Bob said that of course the Club was all very well, but he should insist on Uncle Tom's tossing his things into his grip and coming over to Beacon Hill with him to finish up his Boston visit.

They did not talk about Jean any more that night, but the next morning after breakfast they went at the discussion and were just in the midst of it when who should walk in but Jean herself. She had been spending two or three days with a friend of her mother who lived in the suburbs.

"Uncle Bob!" she called as she dashed her hat and muff down upon the settle in the hall. "Uncle Bob! Oh, I had a perfectly lovely time. And what do you think! Mrs. Chandler has three darling Irish terrier puppies, and she is going to give me one if you are willing that I should have it. You do like puppies, don't you? I know you'd like these anyway; they are so blinky, and fat, and little."

Tossing her coat on top of the hat and muff she ran up the front stairs and into the library.

"Why, Uncle Tom Curtis!" she cried. "Whatever brought you here?"

Fluttering to the big man's side she gave him a prodigious hug and at the same time dropped a butterfly kiss on the top of his shiny bald head. The next instant she was perched on the arm of Uncle Bob's chair, eyeing her two uncles expectantly.

"You both look so hot and so—well, almost cross, you know. What is the matter?"

"We are talking about you, honey," ventured Uncle Bob after a short, uneasy silence.

"About *me*! And it makes you look as solemn and ruffled up as this? Whatever have I done? Did Mrs. Chandler telephone you about the puppy? Don't worry. I do not mind if I don't have it—really I don't."

"No, dear, it wasn't the puppy. You shall have all the puppies you want so far as I'm concerned," Uncle Bob answered, stroking the tiny hand that nestled in his. "No, your Uncle Tom and I were talking about where you are to live."

"But I thought I was to live here."

"I thought so too," agreed Uncle Bob. "Uncle Tom, though,

is not satisfied with that arrangement. He says he wants you to come and live with him."

"But I couldn't leave you, Uncle Bob—you know that; at least, not for all the time. If there were only two of me and I could live with each of you how nice it would be. Of course I'd love to be with Uncle Tom sometimes. Why couldn't I live with one of you part of the time and with the other the rest of the year? I'd rather be here in the summer, though, I think, because it's near the ocean."

How simple the great tangle over which the two men had argued suddenly seemed!

"Jean has settled it herself!" Uncle Tom exclaimed. "It shall be Pittsburgh winters and Boston summers. I wonder we didn't solve it that way in the beginning."

So everybody was pleased. Even Hannah admitted that if that was the best that could be done she would put up with it; but she made Uncle Tom Curtis promise to lay in a big supply of soap.

"You must scrub her face and hands three times a day, and at least once between meals if she is to live in Pittsburgh," remarked she. "And please remember to have the grime soaked out of her white dresses, Mr. Curtis. Borax and a little ammonia will do it," she concluded seriously.

"We will wash not only the clothes in ammonia water, but Jean if you say so, Hannah," promised Uncle Tom.

At this everybody laughed.

Then by and by they had luncheon, and Uncle Tom Curtis said it was a much better meal than he had had at the Club the night before; and Hannah said that maybe Pittsburgh was not so black as it was painted; and Uncle Bob said he'd send the inside man to the Chandlers' to get the puppy that very afternoon. And he did. And the puppy came, and he was very small, and very fat, and very wobbly. His head was much too large for him and so were his feet.

"You must name him Beacon Hill and call him Beacon for short, Jean," said Uncle Tom Curtis—which, coming from Uncle Tom Curtis, who thought there was no place on earth like Pittsburgh, was a generous condescension.

CHAPTER II

JEAN HAS A SURPRISE
AND GIVES ONE

NCLE TOM CURTIS returned to Pittsburgh the next day, leaving Jean and Beacon to stay with Uncle Bob until October. It was now April, and on the Common and Public Garden the trees, which were beginning to break into delicate foliage, were invaded by scores of scampering gray squirrels so tame that they would eat out of one's hand. Often in the morning when Jean walked to the office with Uncle Bob she would stop to feed these hungry little creatures and also the flocks of friendly pigeons clustering along the walks. Of course Beacon had to be left behind when the family went on such strolls, for he was far too fond of chasing everything he saw; afternoon was his gala time. Then, while Jean flew on roller skates along the broad asphalt Esplanade bordering the Charles River, Beacon would race up and down dodging the skaters, playing with the children, and nearly tripping up the throngs of nurse-maids who trundled their wee charges in the bright sunshine.

How quickly the days passed!

Already the Beacon Hill house had become a real home, and Uncle Bob dearer each moment she stayed in it.

"You know, Uncle Bob, you would be really perfect if only you liked dolls and could tie hair ribbons," said Jean teasingly.

Uncle Bob shook his head ruefully.

"I never could care for sawdust people," said he, "when there were so many interesting real ones in the world. As for the hair ribbons, perhaps I might learn to tie those in time, although I doubt if I ever could make as perky a bow as Hannah does. I like the *perk* but I haven't the faintest idea how to get it."

Jean laughed.

She and her uncle had many a joke together.

"He is better at a joke than Uncle Tom is," confided Jean to Hannah.

In fact Uncle Bob joked so much that it was hard to tell when he was serious, and so one day when he came into the library where Jean was and swept all the dolls on the couch over into the corner, laughingly demanding how Jean would like to go to Europe, she paid no attention to him.

"Seems to me you are not a very enthusiastic or grateful young woman," said he at last tweaking a curl that hung low on her cheek. "Here I am inviting you to tour the world with me and all you say is: 'I'll think about it!' How's that for gratitude?"

"If you had any intention of taking me I might be more grateful," Jean answered, fastening the gown of the doll she was dressing, and holding her at arm's length to enjoy the effect.

"But I am entirely serious, my young friend; I never was

more so. I am imploring you to go to Italy, for go I must, and I have no mind to leave you behind."

"To Italy? To real Italy, Uncle Bob? Do you mean it?"

"I surely do, dear child. Behold me, solemn as an owl. Ah, now you begin to listen. It would serve you right if I should refuse to take such an ungrateful lady. What say you? Should you like to go?"

"Like it! I'd love it! I've never been on an ocean trip in all my life."

"You may not care to go on another after you've been on this one," chuckled Uncle Bob. "However, the fact remains that we are going. I have charge of decorating a very beautiful house in the suburbs and I am going over to Florence to order some marble stairways and fireplaces. That is my excuse. Incidentally we can make a pleasant trip out of it and see many places besides Italy."

"Could we go to Venice?" burst out Jean. "Venice is in Italy, isn't it? I'd like of all places to see Venice with its water streets and its gondolas."

"Yes, honey, you certainly shall see Venice and ride in all the gondolas you like."

"Splendid!" cried Jean, clapping her hands. "When can we start? Let's go right away," and springing up from the couch she whirled toward the door.

"Slowly, slowly!" protested Uncle Bob. "Come back here to me a moment, you flyaway. Many things must be decided before we sail for Italy. In the first place there is Hannah; what shall we do with her?"

"Oh, Hannah must come along with us," Jean answered. "She'll have to. We never could think of going to Europe and leaving good old Hannah, who is so kind to both of us, now could we? Besides, she has to fix my hair every morning, and mend my clothes. I'd be coming to pieces all over Europe if Hannah didn't go."

"Well, then, that settles it. Hannah goes. I never could consent to escort a young lady who might drop to pieces at any moment and strew her belongings all along the route from Italy to Scotland. Now about Esther, the waitress. She wants to go West and visit her brother; this will be just the chance. Suppose we tie a long string to her and let her go. Then we come to Beacon."

"Beacon would go with us, of course," Jean replied quickly. "You may be sure I'd never leave Beacon at home. I'd rather not go myself."

"But, girlie, we couldn't very well——"

"Why, Uncle Bob! You don't mean to say you thought of leaving Beacon! If you did I simply sha'n't go. That's all there is about it. I shall never, never be parted from Beacon—never!"

"Listen, dear. Beacon wouldn't enjoy going. We could not get for him the food to which he is accustomed, nor would they admit him to the picture galleries which we shall visit. I doubt if he would even care for the gondolas."

"No, I'm sure he would not like the gondolas," admitted Jean smiling faintly, "because Hannah and I tried him on the swan-boats in the Public Garden and he hated them; he just barked and snarled all the time, and wriggled about so in my arms that he nearly went overboard and carried me with him."

"That's just it! That is precisely the way he would feel on shipboard. Now my plan is this. We'll send him out to Pittsburgh for Uncle Tom to take care of until you get back. Then when you go out there in October your doggie will be nicely settled in his other home and waiting for you. In fact," confessed Uncle Bob a little sheepishly, "I wrote Uncle Tom and asked how he would feel about adding a puppy to his household. This is his answer:

"'European plan excellent. Send Beacon. Next best thing to Jean.'"

"Dear Uncle Tom! He is awfully good, isn't he?"

"Yes, he is. I fancy he will decide so, too, when he finds all his sofa cushions torn, and his shoes chewed up," chuckled Uncle Bob. "Let him take his turn at it."

Beacon provided for, the remainder of the European plan seemed simple enough. To be sure there was Hannah, who at first flatly refused to be separated from the golden dome of the State House or from the Boston "Evening Transcript." At last, however, after much persuasion she consented to suffer these deprivations for the common good, and brought herself to purchasing the necessary clothing for Jean and herself. To these she added French, German and Italian dictionaries because, as she explained: "We might get lost or parted from your Uncle Bob somehow, and you never can tell what will happen in those heathen countries where the poor people cannot speak English. How men and women can live in places where they talk those dreadful languages and use that queer money when they might come over here to Boston——"

"That's right, Hannah," agreed Uncle Bob, playfully urging her on.

"And all that strange weather! Why, I read only the other day that in Italy they just have summer all the year round. So foolish! They never get any snow at all—think of that! It is such a slack and lazy way to do always to be wearing one set of things and never getting out any winter flannels. I shouldn't know where I was if I didn't chalk off the seasons by my house cleaning, preserving, getting out the furs, and putting them away. I just know those Italians live without any system. How could they be expected to have any when it's summer all the time?"

She sniffed scornfully.

In fact Hannah sniffed a good many times before the great ship which was carrying them to Naples docked beneath the shadow of Vesuvius. The staterooms she termed little coops, and the berths nothing more nor less than shelves.

"When I go to bed, Mr. Bob, I feel exactly as if I was a sheet put away in the linen closet."

Uncle Bob and Jean both laughed. Hannah kept them royally entertained.

"As for these clocks that strike every hour but the right one—I've nothing to say," she went on. "If the captain prefers to ring two when he means nine, well and good. He runs the ship and it is his lookout, although I will say it is hard on the rest of us. He explains that it has something to do with the watch—whose watch I don't know; his own, I suppose. Evidently he has some queer way of telling time, some theory he is free to work out when he is here in the middle of the ocean away from land. Be glad, Jean, that you learned to tell time properly, and that you live with people who are content to use the old method and do not set themselves up to invent a system that is a puzzle to every one but themselves."

Thus Hannah measured every new experience, applying to it the Beacon Hill standard. If it conformed to what was done in Boston it was quite correct, but if it varied in the least it was condemned as "ridiculous."

To Jean, on the contrary, the voyage was one of unending delight. She proved herself an excellent sailor, and was never tired of playing shuffle-board on the deck or pacing to and fro with Uncle Bob in the fresh breeze. And when at last Gibraltar was reached and she actually beheld the coasts of Spain, Africa and Italy, her wonder grew until she said she had to pinch herself to be sure she was alive and not dreaming. It was a journey of marvels.

"I feel exactly as if I had gone down the rabbit hole with Alice," she exclaimed, squeezing Uncle Bob's arm as they were disembarking at Naples.

Uncle Bob was in such a hurry to reach Florence that the travelers did not stay long in Naples—only long enough to visit the famous Aquarium with its myriad of strange sea creatures, and to take a flying glimpse of the Museum. It was at the latter place that Jean saw the celebrated Naples Vase which, Uncle Bob told her, was found over a hundred years ago in a tomb in Pompeii.

"It probably was made by very skilful Grecian workmen about the year 70 A.D. Think how wonderful it is that there were artists living many thousands of years ago who knew how to make such a beautiful thing. Look closely at it, Jean, for it is one of the art treasures of the world."

Jean looked.

The vase, scarcely more than a foot in height, was of dark blue glass, and had upon it in white a design of delicate Grecian figures.

"It was first made with a coating of white opaque glass entirely over the blue," Uncle Bob explained. "Then the artist with extreme care and some sharp instrument cut this beautiful picture of the harvest gatherers. Notice, too, how the pattern is repeated on the handles. It is a pity the base or foot of the vase is missing; it was probably of gold and was doubtless stolen at some time. There is now made in England a kind of pottery called Wedgwood, which has much this same effect although, of course, it is far less perfectly fashioned."

"I'm glad I do not have this thing to dust," Hannah observed grimly.

"Well you may be, Hannah," Uncle Bob retorted, "for the vase is worth thousands of dollars. There are in the world several very famous glass vases—this is one; the Auldjo Vase, also from Pompeii and now in the British Museum, is another; and the Portland Vase, which is there too, makes a third. The design on the Portland Vase is considered even finer than this. We shall see it and I will tell you its history when we get to London."

What weren't they to see!

Jean's head was a jumble of fairy anticipations—of Crown Jewels, palaces, gondolas, famous pictures, and scenes of undreamed of beauty. The Tower of London merged itself with visions of Napoleon's Tomb, while in and out of her mind flitted fragmentary pictures of Notre Dame and the Vatican. Everything seemed so old!

"At first I stood with my mouth open when I was told things were built, or dug up, or made hundreds of years ago," laughed Jean. "But now I find I am growing fussy, and unless a thing is thousands of years old it scarcely seems worth looking at. How horribly new they must think us in America! Even Bunker Hill and the State House, Hannah, are very modern," she added teasingly.

"Now, Jean, if this trip to Europe is going to make you turn up your nose at your native land the best thing you can do is to face round and go straight back home," was Hannah's severe reply.

"There, there, you dear old thing! Don't worry. I love my America, but you should have learned by this time that I never can resist seeing you bristle. But even you, biased as you are, must admit that a great deal seems to have happened in the world before we on the other side of the sea were alive at all."

"Much of it," observed Hannah with dignity, "was nothing to be proud of, and it's as well they kept it on this side of the ocean."

From Naples Uncle Bob whirled his bewildered charges to Rome and then to Florence, and while he was busy transacting business Hannah and Jean were put in charge of a courier and taken to see so many pictures and churches that Hannah begged never to be shown another masterpiece or another spire so long as she lived.

"Bless your heart, Mr. Bob, if you were to lean the Sistine Madonna right up against the table in my room I wouldn't turn my head to look at it. And as for churches—I wouldn't accept Westminster Abbey as a gift. Tell 'em not to urge it on me, for I wouldn't take it even if I could get it through the customs free of duty. The things I'd like best at this very minute would be an east wind and some baked beans."

But when they reached Venice and saw their first gondola even Hannah was forced to admit that it far outshone the Boston swan-boats. The travelers arrived late at night, and on passing through the station came out on a broad platform where, instead of cabs and cars, numberless gondolas floated, illumined by twinkling lights.

"Oh!" murmured Jean in a hushed whisper.

It was indeed a beautiful sight. Before them a stretch of water flooded by the full moon wandered off into a multitude of tiny canals shut in on either side by murky dwellings of stone or brick. In and out of these dim little avenues plied boatmen who shouted a warning in shrill Italian as they rounded the turns.

Uncle Bob lost no time in summoning a gondolier, and soon the party were being swept along by the sturdy strokes of a swarthy Venetian who, Hannah declared in an undertone, looked like nothing so much as a full-fledged brigand. She could not be persuaded to take her hand off her luggage, but sat clutching it with all her strength until she arrived at the hotel. Jean, on the other hand, was too excited by the novelty of the scene to know or care what the boatman looked like. Her one fear seemed to be that if she went to bed and allowed herself to fall asleep the wonderful water streets might vanish forever. It took all Uncle Bob's pleading to make her close her eyes. At last, however, she did and when she opened them in the morning her very first thought was to fly to the window and see if the canals were still there.

No, it was not a dream!

There were the moving gondolas, the narrow water streets, and the glorious dome of Del Salute directly opposite across the sparkling expanse of the Grand Canal.

Jean suppressed a cry of delight, and scurried into her clothes.

"Now, Uncle Bob," she announced at breakfast, "I want to go straight out in a gondola the minute I have finished my chocolate and rolls. I think I am pretty good to stop for them at all. I want to go and stay until noon. May I?"

"Well, let me think a second, little girl," replied Uncle Bob. "I am afraid I must run over to the bankers' directly after breakfast, so I won't be able to start right away; I can, however, take you later." Then as he saw Jean's face fall he added, "You and Hannah may go early if you like and come back for me at eleven. How will that do?"

"It will do beautifully only I wish you could be with us. How shall we know how to get a boatman, or tell him where to take us? I am sure I couldn't, and Hannah's Italian is not very good, although," with a mischievous smile, "I suppose she could use her dictionary."

"I will arrange everything with a gondolier before I leave for the bankers'," Uncle Bob answered. "Now I must be running along. Suppose the gondola is here at half-past nine."

"The earlier the better," cried Jean.

Promptly at the hour set the gondola glided up to the steps of the Grand Canal Hotel where Jean and Hannah were waiting. It was an unusually beautiful gondola, with scarlet curtains and a gilded prow carved in the shape of a woman's head.

Jean sprang forward, all eagerness, her eyes on the magic apparition. Then suddenly her foot slipped on the slime left by the tide on the marble step, and she would have fallen into the water had not a young boy, with rare presence of mind, leaped forward and caught her.

Another moment and Hannah, white with fright, had the girl in her arms.

"Oh, my dear child!" she wailed. "My precious lamb! Thank goodness, you are safe. Think if you'd been drowned before you had had a chance to see Venice at all! But you are quite safe now, honey. Don't be frightened. Young man," and she turned to the boy, "that was a good deed of yours. What is your name? But there—how silly to be asking him when he can't understand a word I'm saying. I forgot no one could understand anything in this queer, upside-down town where the streets are water when they ought to be land."

To her utter astonishment, however, the boy answered in English, which, although slightly broken, was perfectly intelligible.

"My name is Giusippe Cicone."

"Say it again," demanded Hannah. "Say it more slowly."

"Giusippe Cicone."

"Giusippe," echoed Hannah, "Giusippe Cicone. There! Giusippe Cicone. I got it better that time. Giusippe Cicone. Now I have it! Well, Master Giusippe Cicone, it was very good of you to save this little lady from a ducking in your canal which, if I may be permitted to say so, is not as clean as it might be. We are very much obliged to you, and here is some money to pay you for being so quick."

The boy shook his head.

"I could not take money for saving the señorita from the water," protested he proudly. "I was glad to do it. I could not take pay."

"Well, I thank you very much," Jean ventured shyly.

He helped Hannah and the girl into the waiting gondola and then stood on the steps shading his eyes with his brown hand as the gondolier made his way to the oar.

"Perhaps you can tell us where we can find you if we should want to see you again," called Hannah as the distance between them widened.

"Certainly. I am at Murano." He pointed across the lagoon to a distant island.

"EVERY ONE KNOWS ME AT THE GLASS WORKS"

"Murano?"

"Yes, I work there. Every one knows me at the glass works."

He waved his hand and was soon lost to sight.

"I do wonder who he is," speculated Jean, who had now quite recovered from her fright and could smile at the memory of the episode. "And how strange that he understood English!"

"I don't call it strange," Hannah responded. "English is the only sensible language, and probably this boy realizes it. I think it speaks well for his discrimination."

"Anyway, he was a gentleman not to take the money; and yet he looked poor," reflected the girl.

"One may be a gentleman despite poverty, thank goodness," Hannah said. "Your uncle will probably insist upon hunting him up and thanking him. I can't see, Jean, how you came to slip that way. Wasn't the boatman holding on to you?" and for the tenth time every detail of the disaster had to be gone over.

"Well, all I can say is that if anything had happened to you I never should have dared show my face to your Uncle Bob. And think of your Uncle Tom at home—he would have things to say! They would both blame me even if it was not my fault," sighed Hannah.

"Of course it wasn't your fault. How could you possibly be to blame if I was so heedless as to rush ahead without looking where I was going? I'm always doing that, Hannah; you know I am. I am always in such a hurry to enjoy the things I like that I never can wait a moment. This is a good lesson for me. I just hope the salt water won't spoil my new tan shoes. Come! Let us talk of something pleasanter. Isn't it too perfectly lovely out here? Look back at the shore and see how St. Mark's and the Campanile stand out. I know those already, because I remember seeing pictures of them in my geography. Oh, I am so glad we are here! I am sure we shall have a wonderful time in Venice even if I did begin by nearly drowning myself in the canal."

"It is all very well to laugh about it now," Hannah answered solemnly, "but it was no laughing matter when it happened— no laughing matter!"

CHAPTER III

GIUSIPPE TELLS A STORY

WHEN Uncle Bob heard of Jean's adventure he lost no time, you may be sure, in hunting up Giusippe Cicone. A note was sent to Murano asking that the lad call at the hotel; and as the lowing day chanced to be a festa day the glass works were closed and Giusippe presented himself directly after breakfast. He was neatly although poorly clothed, and had he had no other claim to Mr. Cabot's good will than his frank face that would have won him a welcome. Perhaps added to Uncle Bob's gratitude there was, too, a measure of the artist's joy in the beautiful; for Giusippe was handsome. Thick brown hair clustered about the well-formed head; his eyes were of soft hazel; and into his round olive cheek was steeped the rich crimson of the southern sun. More than all this, he was a well bred lad—manly, courteous, and proud. When Mr. Cabot began to thank him for his service to Jean the boy made light of what he had done and once more refused to accept any reward.

Uncle Bob's curiosity was aroused.

Never before had he met an Italian who would not take money when it was offered him.

"Perhaps you would be willing, young man, to tell us more about yourself," said he at last. "You work in the glass factory, you say. Have you been long there?"

Giusippe smiled, showing two rows of dazzling white teeth.

"So long, señor, that I cannot remember when I was not there. And before me was my father, and my grandfather; and before that his father; and so on back for years and years. There was always a Cicone at Murano. For you must know, señor, that glass-making has ever been the great art of Venice. When paintings began to take the place of the glass mosaics then came the height of fame for Venetian glass. For you will remember that for many years before artists could paint people made pictures out of bits of glass, and in this way represented to those who had no books scenes from the Bible or from history. Then wonderful painters were born in Italy and they crowded out the mosaic makers, who had previously decorated the churches, palaces, and public buildings. The making of glass mosaics died out and it was then that the Venetian artisans turned their attention and their skill to the making of other glass things—beads, mirrors, drinking cups, and ornaments. In fact," went on Giusippe, "there soon became so many glass houses in Venice that the Great Council feared a terrible fire might sweep the island, and in 1291, with the exception of a few factories for small articles, all the glass houses were banished to the island of Murano a mile distant where, if fire came, no destruction could be done to the city of Venice itself. Those factories which were allowed to remain had to have a space of fifteen paces around them. By the decree of the Council the other glass houses were torn down."

"And it was thus that your great-great-great-great-great-grandfather was driven to Murano, was it?" queried Mr. Cabot.

"Yes. He was a member of the guild of bead-makers. For you know, señor, that in those days workmen were banded together in guilds, and kept the mysteries of their trade to themselves. The precious secret was handed down from father to son. So it was with my great-great-great-great-great-grandfather."

Giusippe drew himself up.

"Oh, it was a grand thing to be a glass-maker in those days, señor!" continued the boy, his eyes glowing. "The members of the guilds were so honored in Venice that they were considered equal in birth to the noblest families. They were gentlemen. A titled woman felt only pride in uniting herself with a glass-maker's family."

"Perhaps that is what your great-great-great-great-great-grandmother did," Jean said, half aloud.

"Yes, señorita," was Giusippe's simple answer. "And they say, too, she was beautiful. My ancestor was of the *pater-nostereri*; he was a maker of beads for rosaries. Then there were the *margaritai*, who made small beads; and the *fuppialume*, who made large blown beads. Each man was a skilled artist, you see, and did some one special thing. The *phiolari* made vases, cups, and glass for windows; the *cristallai* optical glass; and the *specchiai* mirrors. No strangers were allowed to visit the glass works, and all apprentices must pass a rigid examination not only as to their skill, but as to their previous personal history. In 1495 the glass houses at Murano extended for a mile along a single street and the great furnaces roared night and day, so you can imagine how much glass was made on the island."

"My!" gasped Jean breathlessly.

"Absolute loyalty to the art was demanded of every man engaged in it," Giusippe said. "And you can see, señor, that this was necessary. Any workman carrying the secrets elsewhere was first warned to return to Venice; then, if he refused, his nearest relative was imprisoned; if he still refused to obey he was tracked down and killed. Often glass-makers were found in Padua, Ravenna, and other places stabbed through the heart, and the word *Traitor* was fastened to the dagger."

Jean shuddered.

"Do not tremble, señorita," Giusippe said. "It was a just punishment. You see the Council of Ten felt that the prosperity of the Venetians depended upon keeping their art away from all the outside world which was so eager to learn it. All knew the penalty for disloyalty. The decree read:

"'If any workman conveys his art to a strange country to the detriment of the Republic he shall be sent an order to return to Venice. Failing to obey his nearest of kin shall be imprisoned. If he still persists in remaining abroad and plying his art an emissary shall be charged to kill him.'

"In this way the secrets of glass-making were kept in Venice and the Republic soon became famous and prosperous. As the reputation of the Venetian glass-makers spread an immense trade was established. My grandfather has often told me of the great numbers of beads which were sent everywhere throughout the East—sometimes to Africa and even to India. In 1764 twenty-two great furnaces were kept busy supplying the beads that were demanded. Frequently, they say, as many as forty-four thousand barrels were turned out in a single week."

"Why, I should think that everybody in the world would have been covered with beads!" Jean exclaimed, smiling.

"Ah, I can tell you something stranger than that, señorita. So popular did Venetian glass of every variety become that a foreign prince created a great sensation by appearing in Paris with curls of finely spun black glass."

Jean and Uncle Bob laughed merrily.

"I think myself he was silly," Giusippe declared, echoing their amusement. "He, however, was not alone in his admiration for the beautiful and ingenious workmanship of the people of my country, for even as far back as 1400 Richard the Second of England gave permission to our Venetian merchants to sell glass aboard their galleys, duty free; and King Henry the Eighth owned as many as four or five hundred Venetian drinking goblets, vases, dishes, and plates, some of which, they say, are still in the British Museum."

"We must see them when we go to London, mustn't we, Uncle Bob?" cried Jean eagerly.

"We surely must. All this is very interesting, Giusippe. You do well to remember so much of your country's history," said Mr. Cabot.

"I am proud of it, señor. Besides I have heard it many, many times. My people were never tired of telling over and over the story of the old days; the golden days of Venice, my father called them. The Republic might have retained its fame much longer had not some of our countrymen been persuaded to go to other lands and sell their secrets for gold. It was thus that the art of making mirrors was taken into France and Germany."

"Tell us about it, Giusippe," pleaded Jean.

"Why, as I think I told you, the Venetians began to make mirrors as early as 1300. Of course, señorita, they were crude affairs—not at all like the fine ones of to-day, but to people who had nothing better they were marvels. And indeed they were both clever and beautiful. For you must remember that ages ago there was no such thing as a looking-glass. Men and women could only see their reflections in streams, pools, and fountains. Then the Egyptians, Greeks, and Romans began to make mirrors of burnished metal, using bits of brass or bronze often beautifully decorated on the back with classic Grecian figures. Rich women carried such mirrors fastened to their girdles or sometimes instead had them fitted into small, shallow boxes of carved ivory; sometimes too the mirror was set in a case of gold, silver, enamel, or ebony with intricate decoration on the outside. That was the first of mirror-making."

"How curious!"

"Later the Venetians experimented and began backing pieces of glass with mercury or tin. The surface was first covered with tinfoil and then rubbed down until smooth; then the whole was coated with quicksilver, which formed an amalgam with the tin. It does no harm to tell you about it now, señorita," added Giusippe a little sadly, "for every one knows. This process was slow and unsatisfactory, but it was the best the workmen then knew. These mirrors they set in elaborate frames of glass, silver, carved wood, mother-of-pearl, coral, tarsi, or into frames of painted wood. Some of them were sent by Venetian nobles as gifts to kings and queens of other countries; often they were purchased by royalties themselves. You can see many in the museums of France, Germany, or England."

"We will hunt them up, Jean," Uncle Bob declared.

"I'd love to see them," replied the girl.

"My father has told me that there were frequent quarrels between the glass-makers and the mirror-framers because, you see, the framers wanted to learn the secret of making the mirrors, and the mirror-makers were jealous of the skill of the framers and feared the frame would be more beautiful than the mirror itself and so overshadow it. Then in 1600 the French stole from our people the secret of mirror-making and began turning out mirrors not only as good, but in some respects better than the Venetian ones."

"Oh, Giusippe, how did they steal the secret?" Jean cried. "How dreadful!"

"It was through the treachery of our own countrymen, señorita," Giusippe confessed. "Yes, sorry as I am to say so, it was our own fault. The French, you see, as well as the Venetians, had long been experimenting with glass-making and since it was considered there, as here, an art, many penniless Huguenot gentlemen who had lost their fortunes took it up; for one might be a glass-maker and still retain his noble rank. Such was Bernard Palissy——"

"The potter!" interrupted Jean. "I learned all about him in my history."

Giusippe nodded.

"So? Then you know how he struggled for years to solve the secret of making the enamel he had seen on a Saracen cup. Palissy also made some fine old stained glass, although few people seem to know this. Many another Frenchman tried to discover the Venetian's great secret. They sought to bribe our people to tell the process, but without success. Then Colbert, the chief minister under Louis the Fourteenth, wrote the French ambassador at Venice that he must obtain for France some Venetian workmen. The ambassador was upset enough, as you may imagine, when he received the order. He said he could not do it. He dared not. If found out he would be thrown into the sea."

"He ought to have been!" Jean cried. "He would have deserved it."

"I think so too," Uncle Bob agreed.

"It would have been far better for Venice had he been drowned in the Adriatic," Giusippe answered slowly. "But he wasn't. Instead he began cautiously to look about. There are always in the world, señor, men who have no pride in their fatherland and can be bought with money. The next year the ambassador succeeded in bribing eighteen glass-makers to go to France and make mirrors for Versailles, the palace of the French king. And no sooner had these men got well to work and passed the mystery on to the French than Colbert forbade the French people to import any more mirrors from Venice, as mirrors could now be made at home. Some of these early French mirrors are now in the Cluny Museum in France, my father told me. In consequence of the treachery of these workmen Germany also soon learned how to make mirrors, and the fame of the Venetian artisans declined just as the Council had predicted it would. But it will be long before any other country can equal mine in the making of filigree or spun glass. You will, señorita, see much of this beautiful work while you are here in Venice."

"I want to, Giusippe; and I want to get some to take home. May I, Uncle Bob?"

Mr. Cabot nodded.

"Your story is like a fairy tale, Giusippe," said he.

The boy smiled with pleasure.

"It is a wonderful story to me because it is the story of my people. And, señor, there is much more to tell, but I must not weary you. Some of our filigree glass, it is true, became too elaborate to be beautiful. It is simply interesting because it is wonderful that out of glass could be fashioned ships, flowers, fruits, fish, and decorations of all kinds. It shows most delicate workmanship. But the drinking glasses with their fragile stems are really beautiful; and so are the vases and tazzas from white glass with enamel work or filigree of delicately blended colors. It was the Venetians, too, who invented engraved glass, where a design is scratched or cut into the surface with a diamond or steel point of a file. And our mille-fiori glass, which came to us way back from the Egyptians, is another famous variety. This is made from the ends of fancy colored sticks of glass cut off and arranged in a pattern. You will see it in the shops here."

"I think you Venetians are wonderful!" Jean exclaimed.

"Ah, señorita, you have yet to see one of the finest things we have done," was Giusippe's grave reply. "You have to see the San Marco with its mosaics!"

"Yes, we surely want to go there," put in Mr. Cabot. "Do you think you could be our guide, Giusippe?"

"I could go to-morrow, señor; because of the festa I am

free from work. I would like to show you San Marco, of all things, because I love it."

"I am sure no one could do it better," replied Mr. Cabot, well pleased. "To-morrow at nine, then. We will be ready promptly. You shall tell us the rest of your fascinating Venetian history and make Venetians of us."

"I will come, señor."

"You shall be paid for your time, my boy."

"Alas, señor! That would spoil it all. I could not then show it to you. Forgive me and do not think me ungrateful. But my San Marco is to me the place I love. I show it to you because I love it. I have played about it and wandered in and out its doors since I was a very little child. I am proud that you should see it, señor."

"As you will. To-morrow then."

"Yes, señor."

Another moment and Giusippe was gone.

"A remarkable boy! A most remarkable boy!" ejaculated Mr. Cabot. "He knows his country's history as I fancy few others know it. Could you pass as good an examination on yours, Jean?"

Jean hung her head.

"I'm afraid not."

"Nor I," Uncle Bob remarked, patting her curls kindly.

CHAPTER IV

UNCLE BOB ENLARGES HIS PARTY

I N accordance with his promise Giusippe came promptly the next morning and the four set out for the San Marco. It was a beautiful June day. The piazza was warm with sunshine, and as groups of tourists loitered through it the pigeons circled greedily about their feet begging food.

"Why, Uncle Bob, these pigeons are exactly like the ones at home—just as pretty and just as hungry," Jean said.

"Should you like to stop a moment and feed them, little girl?"

"Oh, do! It will make Hannah think of Boston," begged Jean. "But we have nothing to give them," she added in dismay.

"I will find you something, señorita," Giusippe declared.

Darting up to an old Italian who was standing near he soon returned with a small paper cornucopia filled with grain.

"The pigeons of St. Mark's are very tame. See!"

He put some kernels of corn on the top of his hat, and holding more in his outstretched hands stood motionless.

There was a whirr of wings, and in an instant the boy was quite hidden beneath an eager multitude of fluttering whiteness.

"I never saw so many pigeons," Jean whispered. "You have many more than we do at home."

"We Venetians are very fond of the birds," was Giusippe's reply. "So, too, are the tourists who come to Venice, for they never seem to be tired of having their pictures taken surrounded by flocks of pigeons."

"Doesn't this make you think of Boston Common, Hannah?" asked Uncle Bob.

"Yes, a little. But I should feel more as if I were in Massachusetts if there were not such a babel of foreign tongues about me." Then turning to Giusippe she demanded: "How did you come to speak English, young man?"

"I have been expecting you would ask me that," smiled Giusippe. "You see, I have an uncle who went to America; yes, to Pennsylvania, to seek his fortune. He stayed there five years and in that time he learned to speak English well. When he came back he taught me all he knew. Then he returned with his wife to the United States, and I got books and studied. When they found at Murano that I could speak English they often called on me to show tourists over the glass works. In this way I picked up many words and their pronunciation. Since then I have found that I could sometimes serve as interpreter for English or American travelers if I watched for the chance. I was eager for such opportunities, for it gave me practice, and I often learned new words."

"And why are you so anxious to learn English, Giusippe?" Jean questioned.

"I hope, señorita, to go some day to the United States. My

uncle told me what a wonderful country it is, and I desire to see it. Perhaps in that beautiful great land where everything is in abundance I might grow rich. I now have nothing to keep me here; my parents are dead and I have no other kinsmen. I want to join my uncle in Pennsylvania as soon as I have enough money. Part of my passage I have already saved."

"Why, Giusippe!"

"Yes, señorita, I am in earnest. It is lonely here in Venice now that I have no people. And Murano is not what it was in the golden days of my ancestors. I am sure I could find work in your country if I should go there. Do you not think I could, señor?" He turned to Mr. Cabot.

"It is possible," was Uncle Bob's thoughtful answer. "Especially since you speak English so well. What sort of thing would you like to do?"

"I know my trade of glass-making," was Giusippe's modest answer. "I know, too, much of coloring stained glass and of mosaic making. These things I have known from my babyhood up. There must be such work for persons going to the United States. Perhaps my uncle, who is in Pittsburgh with a large glass company, could get me something to do there."

"Pittsburgh!" exclaimed the other three in a breath.

"Yes. My uncle is with the company of a Señor Thomas Curtis, who has been very kind to him."

"Uncle Tom! It's Uncle Tom!" Jean cried, laying her hand impulsively on his arm. "Mr. Curtis is my uncle, Giusippe. Did you ever hear anything so wonderful!"

"It certainly is a strange coincidence," agreed Mr. Cabot. "But why did your uncle come back, Giusippe, after he once got over there?"

"Ah, it was this way. He went first alone, expecting when he had enough money to send it back so that the young girl he loved could follow him, and they could be married. But when at last he had the money saved her parents became sick. They were old people. She could not leave them to die here alone, señor. Therefore she refused to go to America, and so much did my uncle love Anita that he would not stay there without her. Back he came and worked once more at Murano. Then the father and mother died, and my uncle and Anita were married and went to the United States. They wanted to take me, but I pretended that I would rather remain here. This I did because I feared that if I went with them and did not find work I might be a burden. All this was several years ago. My uncle is now a superintendent in one of the Curtis glass factories, and is happy and prosperous. Still, there are children, and I could not let him pay my fare to America. As I said, it will not take me much longer to save the rest of my passage money. Then I shall go and perhaps become rich. Who knows, señor!" Giusippe broke into a ringing laugh.

Mr. Cabot made no reply.

He was thinking.

Fearing that he had offended, Giusippe changed the subject.

"But I weary you with my affairs, señor. Pardon. Shall we go on to St. Mark's?"

It was but a few steps across the piazza, and they were soon inside the church. Then for the first time Mr. Cabot spoke.

"This church, Jean," said he, "is the link between the old art of the Mohammedans and the Gothic art of the Christian era. It was planned as a Byzantine church, and in it one can see many things suggesting St. Sofia's at Constantinople. When

St. Mark's at Alexandria was destroyed by the Mohammedans many of its treasures fell into the hands of the Doge of Venice, who promptly proclaimed St. Mark the new patron saint in place of St. Theodore and set about building a cathedral in which to put all the beautiful things he had acquired. Some parts of this ancient cathedral remain, but most of the church was built by Doge Contarini between 1063 and 1071. To the next Doge, Domenico Selvo, fell the task of decorating it. You see, over here the building of churches takes longer than it does at home."

"I should think it did," answered Jean. "Why, we think it is awful if our churches are not all done in two years."

Giusippe smiled.

"Ah, we build not that way here, señorita," he said. "Three centuries did our people spend in building into St. Mark's the marble carvings brought from the East; erecting the altars; and adorning the walls. These mosaics alone it took work-men two hundred and fifty years to fashion. Venice was a rich Republic, you see, and could well afford to put into this cathedral the money she might have spent on war. Above the slabs of marble are the mosaics, señorita. So it was in St. Sofia, my father told me; the slabs of marble near the ground and the decoration above. This whole cathedral of ours is covered on all the walls with mosaics—pictures made from bits of glass put together to form scenes from the Bible or from history. Even the most ignorant people who had had no schooling could read such stories, could they not?"

Jean nodded.

She was dazzled by the beauty of the place—by the soft light; the walls rich in gold and color; by the many wonderful things there were to be seen. She was interested, too, in the smoothly worn, uneven floor which showed where the piles beneath the church had settled.

"Mosaic makers, you know, Jean, began crude attempts at making pictures in glass thousands of years ago, for glass-making was familiar to the Egyptians as well as to the Phœnicans and Syrians. The Greeks and Romans, too, were great glass-makers. So glass-making came down through the ages. The Byzantine churches usually were lighted by a row of tiny glass windows round the base of the dome. Some of this ancient glass still remains in St. Sofia. The common way of making such windows was to cut a design in a slab of marble or plaster, and then insert small pieces of colored glass. Sometimes, too, a pattern for wall decoration was worked out by sticking fragments of glass into soft stucco. So the first mosaic work began. We can see some of it in the museums of England."

"There seems to be a great deal to see in those London museums, Uncle Bob," Jean gasped.

"I am afraid you will be more convinced of that fact than ever when you get there," chuckled Uncle Bob. "But to return to Giusippe's mosaics. You may remember, perhaps, that when the Mohammedans invaded Constantinople and found how important a part the glass-makers played in decorating the churches, they at once handed the artisans over to the caliphs, that they might be set to work adorning their mosques. Now the Mohammedans believed it a crime to make a copy of either man or woman in a picture, a carving, or a statue. It was punishable to pay reverence to sacred figures; therefore all decoration in their churches took the form of flowers, fruit, or conventional designs. So no great mosaic pictures with figures such as these were made. Between the thirteenth and fourteenth centuries Damascus became the center of glass-making, and there are in existence in some of the museums old Arab lamps which hung in the mosques with inscriptions from the Koran engraved upon them. It is Giusippe's St. Mark's which revived the art of mosaic making, and served as the bridge between those Pagan days and the days when with Christianity the arts revived and mosaic makers began to represent in glass figures of Christ and the saints."

"And then the painters came, as Giusippe has said," put in Jean.

"Yes, the great artists were born, and from that time pictures on canvas instead of pictures of glass decorated the churches. But the mosaic makers did an important service to art, for it was they who indirectly gave to the world the idea of making stained-glass windows. And in Venice those who ceased to make mosaics made instead the beautiful Venetian glass of which Giusippe has told us."

"And are there no mosaics made now, Uncle Bob?" asked Jean.

"Yes. When in 1858 it became necessary to restore some of the mosaics in St. Mark's, a descendant of one of the old Murano glass workers named Radi, together with a Dr. Salviati, started a factory on the Grand Canal, where they gradually revived some of the past glory of Venice. They copied the old time glass products, making Arab lamps such as hung in the mosques; cameo work similar to the Naples and Portland vases; and pictures in mosaic. It was they who did The Last Supper for Westminster Abbey, and the mosaics for Albert Memorial Hall in London."

"But Salviati's mosaics were not like those here, señor,"

put in Giusippe, "because the San Marco mosaics were constructed upon the walls, small cubes of glass being pressed into the moist cement to make the picture. This gave a rough, irregular surface which artists say is far more artistic than is Salviati's smooth, glassy work. When Salviati sent mosaics away he made them here, and then backed them with cement so they could be placed on a slab of solid material and transported great distances from Venice. His pictures, it is true, were far more perfectly done than were the old mosaics—too perfectly, I have heard glass experts say."

"Undoubtedly they are right, Giusippe, for the roughness in the ancient mosaics would, of course, break up the great plain surfaces and make them more interesting. But Salviati did Venice a service, nevertheless, in reviving the art. And there is, too, another virtue about mosaics, and that is that they will endure far longer than paintings. Had it not been for the foresight of Pope Urban, who between 1600 and 1700 had many of the famous pictures of the Vatican copied in mosaic, these masterpieces would have been lost to the world."

"I have been told that the church in Ravenna has some fine mosaics, but I never have seen them," Giusippe ventured.

"I have. They are beautiful, and I hope you may see them some time. Then there are others scattered through the various churches of Sicily and Rome; and there are also many beautiful inlays of mosaic decorating the old churches and palaces of European cities. When we visit Westminster Abbey, Jean, I must show you the crude early mosaic work on the tomb of Edward the Confessor. It is very curious, for it is made of pieces of colored glass set in grooves of marble."

"How much you are to see, señorita," observed Giusippe wistfully.

Mr. Cabot fixed his eyes attentively on the boy.

"Should you, too, like to see all these wonders, Giusippe?" he asked half playfully and half in earnest.

But Giusippe, who did not catch the banter in his tone, answered seriously:

"Should I? Ah, señor, it is not for me to envy or be unhappy about that which I may not have. Some day, perhaps, when I have made my fortune in your country I can return to the old world and see its marvels. I must have a little patience, that is all."

The mingling of sadness and longing in the reply touched Uncle Bob; Jean and the young Venetian chattered on, but Mr. Cabot walked silently ahead, deep in thought.

"Did I understand you to say, Giusippe," he asked at last turning abruptly, "that you have no relatives in Venice?"

"None in all the world with the exception of the uncle in America of whom I told you, señor."

Again there was a pause.

"Suppose I were to take you with us."

"What, señor?"

"Take you with us now, when we leave Venice."

"I do not understand."

"Suppose I asked you to go with us to France and England, and then across to America."

"But I have not enough money, señor."

"I haven't much, either," Mr. Cabot answered, smiling

kindly into the boy's puzzled eyes. "Still, I think I could get together a sufficient sum to pay your way until you got to the United States and found work."

"To go—to go with you now, do you mean, señor?"

"Yes. We leave Venice next week for France. You see, I like you, Giusippe; we all do. And in addition to that you have done us a service. But more than anything else I feel that, once started, you are capable of making your way and doing well in life; all you need is a chance. I have perfect faith that if I took you to America you would make good. It would cost very little more were you to join us, and no doubt you could help in many little ways during the trip. Do you speak French at all?"

"Yes, some; but more German. It is nothing. Many travelers come to Venice, and one must talk to them. Then, too, here it is not unusual to speak several languages, because the countries lie near together, and the people come and go from place to place. With you it is different; a mighty sea divides you from the rest of the world."

"Despite all your excuses for us, Giusippe, it is quite true that we Americans are as a rule pitiably ignorant about languages. Here is this boy, Jean, who knows not only his mother tongue but French, German and English besides. Isn't that a rebuke to us, with our fine schools and our college educations? It makes me ashamed of myself. Do you, little girl, try and do better than I have. Well, young man, what do you say to my proposition? Will you come with us to America?"

"Señor! Oh, señor! How can I ever——"

"Well, then, that settles it," interrupted Mr. Cabot,

cutting him short. "I will arrange everything. But there is just one condition to be made, my youthful Venetian patriot. If by chance we see any of those old mirrors made by the early Frenchmen who stole your art from Murano you are not to smash them. Remember!"

Giusippe laughed.

CHAPTER V

GIUSIPPE ENCOUN-
TERS AN OLD FRIEND

I T was scarcely a reality to Jean, to Hannah, or to Giusippe himself when Uncle Bob actually set forth for France with the young Venetian as a member of the party. Yet every one was pleased: Hannah because she would not now need her foreign dictionaries; Jean because it was jolly to have a companion her own age; and Giusippe because he felt that at last he had friends who were to guide for him the future which had loomed so darkly and so vaguely before him. Not a full week of the trip to Paris had passed before Mr. Cabot declared that how he had previously got on without that boy he did not understand. Giusippe had such a wonderful way of making himself useful; not only did he see what needed to be done, but he was quick to do it.

"His enthusiasm alone is worth the money I am paying for his railroad fares and hotel bills!" ejaculated Uncle Bob to Hannah.

49

There certainly never was such a boy to take in everything around him, and to remember what he saw. With mind alert for all that was to be learned he tagged along at Mr. Cabot's heels drinking in and storing away every scrap of history and of beauty which came across his path. And in Paris he found much of both. The Invalides with the tomb of Napoleon; Notre Dame with its odd gargoyles; the Arc de Triomphe; the Bois; and the Champs-Elysees shaded by pink horse-chestnut trees—all these sights were new and marvelous to the Italian lad. But it was Versailles with its gardens that charmed him and Jean most.

The travelers arrived there on a Sunday, when the fountains were playing, flowers blooming everywhere, and a gay crowd of sightseers thronging the walks. It was like fairy-land. The great Neptune fountain sent into the air a sheet of spray which was quickly caught up by the sunlight and transformed into a misty rainbow. Within the palace, amid old tapestries of battles and hunting scenes, and surrounded by paintings and statues, were the famous early French mirrors of which Giusippe had previously spoken.

Mr. Cabot pointed them out, half playfully, half seriously.

"Perhaps on further consideration I will leave them," returned the boy, falling in with the spirit of the elder man's mood. "They seem to fit the spaces, and I doubt if even our Venetian mirrors could look better here."

"I think it might be just as well," answered Mr. Cabot. "Besides, you must remember that those mirrors were not the only sort of glass the French made. There were many enamel workers at Provençe as early as 1520, and later much cast glass instead of that which is blown came from France.

In fact, up to a hundred years ago the French held the plate glass monopoly. Then England took up glass-making and cut into the French market—the same old story of stealing the trade, you see. In addition to other varieties of glass-making some of the finest and most interesting of the old stained glass was made by the French people, and can now be seen in the church of St. Denis, just out of Paris, and at Sainte Chapelle which is within the city itself. Fortunately the glass at St. Denis escaped the fury of the French revolutionists, as it might not have done had it not been at a little distance from Paris. There is also glass of much the same sort at Poitiers, Bourges, and Rheims. Amiens, too, has wonderful glass windows. I hope before we leave for home we shall have a peep at some if not all of these."

"Isn't much beautiful French glass now made at Nancy, Mr. Cabot?" Giusippe inquired.

"Yes, some of the finest comes from there."

"But didn't any other people beside the Venetians and the French make glass, Uncle Bob?" asked Jean, much interested.

"Oh, yes. Almost every European nation has tried its hand at glass-making. It is curious, too, to notice how each differs from the others. The Bohemians, for instance, were famous glass-makers, and their work, which primarily imitated that of the Venetians, is known the world over."

"What sort of glass is it? Could I tell it if I should see it?"

"Well, for one thing they make beautiful wine glasses and goblets, having stems of enclosed white and colored enamel tubes twisted together with transparent glass, which look as if they had delicate threads of color running through them. Then the Bohemians and the Austrians make many great beakers or drinking glasses, steins, and bowls with decorative coats of arms upon them in gold or in colored enamel."

"Oh, I have seen things like that," Jean replied.

"Yes, we have some of those ornamental goblets at home in the dining-room. They are very rich and handsome. Beside these varieties the Bohemians have of late revived the making of old white opaque glass with colored enamel figures on it. But engraved glass is one of the kinds for which Bohemia is chiefly celebrated. Even very skilful glass engravers can be had there for little money. They cut fine, delicate designs upon the glass with a lathe. Some of this is white, but much of it is of deep red or blue with the pattern engraved on it in white. Such glass is made in two layers, the outer one being cut away so to leave the design upon the surface underneath."

"Wasn't it the Bohemians who invented cut glass?" Giusippe asked.

"No. Sometimes people say so, but this is not true. The fact is that there chanced to be a glass cutter so skilful that he was appointed lapidary to Rudolph the Second; he had a workshop at Prague, but though he did some very wonderful glass cutting, which gained him much fame, he did not invent the art. It was, by the way, one of his workmen who later migrated to Nuremburg and carried the secret of glass-cutting to Germany."

"Isn't it queer how one country learned of another?" reflected Jean.

"Yes, and it is especially interesting when we see how hard each tried not to teach his neighbor anything. There always was somebody, just as there always is now, who could not keep still and went and told," Mr. Cabot said. "And while we are speaking of the different kinds of glass we must not forget to mention the dark red ruby glass perfected in 1680 by Kunckel, the director of the Potsdam glass works, for it is a very ingenious invention. The deep color is obtained by putting a thin layer of gold between the white glass and the coating of red."

"What else did the Germans make?" queried Giusippe.

"Well, the Germans, like the other nations, turned out glass which was suggestive of their people. And that, by the by, is a fact you must notice when seeing the work of so many different countries. Observe how the art of each reflects the characteristics of those who made it. Italy gave us fragile, dainty glass famous for its airy beauty and delicacy; Germany, on the other hand, fashions a far more massive, rough, and heavier product—large flasks, steins and goblets, some of which are even clumsy; all are substantial and useful, however, and have the big cordial spirit of fellowship so characteristic of the German people. These glasses are decorated in large flat designs less choice, perhaps, than are the Bohemian. The shape of the German goblets and drinking glasses differs, too, from those made in Italy. They are less graceful, less dainty. Instead you will find throughout Germany tall cylindrical shafts, tankards, and steins adorned with massive eagles or colored coats of arms; often, moreover, both the Bohemians and the Germans use pictorial designs showing processions of soldiers, battle scenes, or cavalry charges such as would appeal to nations whose military life has long been one of the leading interests of their people."

"Tell me, Mr. Cabot," inquired Giusippe eagerly, "did you ever see one of the German puzzle cups?"

"Yes, several of them. In the British Museum there are several of the windmill variety."

"What is a puzzle cup, Uncle Bob?" demanded Jean.

"Why, a puzzle or wager cup, as they are sometimes called, was an ingenious invention of the Germans during their early days of glass-making. The kind I speak of is a large inverted goblet which has on top a small silver windmill. The wager was to set the fans revolving, turn the glass right side up, and then fill and drain it before the mill stopped turning. Such wagers were very popular in those olden days and are interesting as relics of a mediæval and far-away period in history."

So intently had Mr. Cabot and the others been talking that they had stopped in the center of the room and it was while they were standing there that a party of tourists entered from the hallway. Foremost among them was an American girl who carried in her hand a much worn Baedeker. As her eye swept over the tapestries covering the walls her glance fell upon Giusippe.

Instantly she started and with parted lips stepped forward; then she paused.

"It cannot be!" Mr. Cabot heard her murmur.

At the same moment, however, Giusippe had seen her.

"The beautiful señorita!" he cried. "My lady of Venice!"

He was beside her in an instant.

"Giusippe! Giusippe!" exclaimed the girl. "Can it really be you?"

"Yes, yes, señorita! It is I. Ah, that I should see you again! What a joy it is. Surely four or five years must have passed since first you came to paint in Venice."

"Fully that, my little Giusippe. It is five years this June. You have a good memory."

"How could I forget you, señorita; and the pictures, and your kindness! But I have left Venice, you see. Yes. Even now I am on my way to America."

"To America? Oh, Giusippe, Giusippe! And that is why you have discarded your faded blouse, and the red tie which you wore knotted round your throat. Alas! I am almost sorry. And yet you look very nice," she added kindly. "But to leave Venice!"

"It is best," Giusippe explained gently. "I have my way to make, and I can do it better in your country, my señorita."

"Perhaps. Still, I am sorry to have you leave your home. It is like taking sea shells away from the sands of the shore."

"And yet you would want me to be a man and succeed in life. Think how you yourself worked for success."

"I know. And it was you who brought it to me, Giusippe. The portrait I painted of you was exhibited in America and when I later sold it to an art dealer there it brought me a little fortune; but the fame it brought was best of all." The girl put her hand softly on the lad's shoulder.

"Oh, señorita, how glad I am!"

"I had a feeling that you would bring me luck the morning when I first saw you in the square near St. Mark's. Do you remember? And how you stood watching me paint? Do you recall how we got to talking and how I asked if I might do the portrait of you? You laughed when I suggested it! And then you came to the hotel evenings when you were free, and I sketched in the picture. It seems but yesterday. In the meantime you entertained me by telling me of Venice and its

"I KNEW HER IN VENICE"

history. What a little fellow you were to know so much!" The girl smiled down at him. "And now let me hear of yourself. What of your parents?"

"Alas, señorita, they have died. I am now quite alone in the world. It is for that that I felt I must leave Venice. It is sad to be alone, señorita."

"So it is, Giusippe. No one knows that better than I." Impulsively she slipped a hand into the small Venetian's. "But I must not take you from your friends. See, we have kept them waiting a long time."

"I want you to meet them, señorita. They are from your country, and they have been kind to me."

"Then surely I must meet them."

With a shy gesture the boy led her forward.

"Miss Cartright is from New York, Mr. Cabot," said Giusippe simply. "Long ago when I was a little lad I knew her in Venice, and she was good to me and to my parents."

"It was five years ago," added Miss Cartright. "I went there to paint."

"And little Giusippe, perhaps, made your stay as delightful as he has made ours," Mr. Cabot said.

"Yes. I was all by myself, and knew no one in Venice. Furthermore, I spoke only a word or two of Italian. Giusippe was a great comfort. He kept me from being lonesome."

"And you are now staying in Paris?" questioned Mr. Cabot.

"Yes, I have been here with friends studying for nearly a year; but I am soon to return home. And now, before I leave you, I want to hear all about Giusippe's plans. What is he to do?"

Little by little the story was told. Mr. Cabot began it and

continued it until Giusippe, who thought him too modest, finished the tale.

"You see, señorita, Mr. Cabot, Miss Jean, and good Hannah will not themselves tell you how kind they have been, so I myself must tell it," said the boy. "And now I go with them to find a position in America that by hard work I may some time be able to repay them for their goodness to me."

Miss Cartright nodded thoughtfully.

At last she said:

"If you should come to New York I want to see you, Giusippe. There might be something I could do to help you. Anyway, I should want to have a glimpse of you. And if you do not come and Mr. Cabot does, perhaps, since he knows how fond of you I am and how much I am interested in your welfare, he will come and tell me how you are getting on."

She drew from her purse a card which she handed to the lad.

"Perhaps I'd better take it, Giusippe," Mr. Cabot said in a low tone. "It might get lost."

Then there was a confusion of farewells, and the girl rejoined her friends, who had gone through into the next room.

It was not until she was well out of ear-shot that any one spoke. Then Jean, who had been silent throughout the entire interview, exclaimed:

"Oh, isn't she beautiful! Isn't she the very loveliest lady you ever saw, Giusippe?"

And Giusippe, answering in voluble English mixed with Italian, extolled not only the fairness but the goodness of his goddess.

Even Hannah agreed that the American girl was charming, but regretted that she had not come from Boston instead of New York.

Uncle Bob alone was silent. Turning the white card in his fingers he stood absently looking at the door through which Miss Ethel Cartright had passed.

CHAPTER VI

UNCLE BOB AS STORY TELLER

NCLE BOB and his party remained in France several weeks, and during that time visited the old French cathedrals with their interesting windows; and saw in the Louvre much glass of early French make as well as many beautiful Venetian mirrors with all sorts of unique histories. One mirror was that famous seventeenth century possession of Marie de Medici, a looking-glass set in a frame which represented a fortune of over thirty thousand dollars. This mirror was of rock crystal combined with cut and polished agates, and around it was a network of enameled gold. Outside this inner frame was a larger one formed entirely of precious stones. Three large emeralds as well as smaller diamonds and rubies adorned it.

"Probably," said Mr. Cabot, "this is but one of many such examples of ancient luxury. Unfortunately, however, most of these extravagant affairs have been melted up by avaricious monarchs who coveted the gems and gold. Such ornate mir-

60

rors are a relic of the Renaissance when each object made was considered an art work on which every means of enrichment was lavished. I do not know that I think it any handsomer than are the simpler mirrors with their Venetian frames of exquisitely carved wood, of which there are many fine specimens in the Louvre."

"Is the mirror that was given by the Republic of Venice to Henry the Third in the Louvre?" asked Giusippe.

"No, that is in the Cluny Museum. You have heard of it, then?"

"Oh, yes; often in Venice. I have seen pictures of it, too," Giusippe replied.

"We must see it before we leave France," declared Mr. Cabot. "It was, as you already know, presented to Henry the Third on his return from Poland. It is set in a wonderfully designed frame of colored and white beveled glass, and the decoration is of alternating fleur-de-lis and palm leaves, which are fastened to the frame by a series of screws. It is quite a different sort of mirror from that of Marie de Medici."

"I should like to see it," Jean said.

"You certainly shall."

How rich France was in beautiful things! One never could see them all.

One of the sights that especially interested Jean and Hannah was the imitation gems displayed in the Paris jewelry shops. These exquisite stones, Uncle Bob told them, were made in laboratories by workmen so skilful that only an expert could distinguish the manufactured gems from the real, the stones conforming to almost every test applied to genuine jewels. They were not manufactured, however, for the purpose of deceiving people, but rather to be sold to those who either could not afford valuable stones or did not wish the care of them. The imitation pearls were especially fine, and by no means cheap either, as Hannah soon found out when she attempted to purchase a small string.

But many as were the wonderful sights in France, the continent had soon to be left behind, and almost before the travelers realized it the Channel had been crossed and they stood upon English soil. As Uncle Bob's time was limited they went direct to London, and when once there one of the first things that Giusippe wished to see were the mosaics in St. Paul's Cathedral of which he had heard so much. So they set out. On reaching the church Giusippe regarded it with awe. How unlike it was to his well loved St. Mark's. And yet how beautiful!

"These mosaics, like the ones we shall see at the Houses of Parliament, were not first made and then put up on the walls as were those such as Salviati and other Venetians shipped from Venice," explained Mr. Cabot. "No, these were made directly upon the walls, the pieces of glass being pressed into prepared areas of cement spread thickly upon the brickwork of the building. The designs are simple, large and effective figures being preferred to smaller and more intricate patterns. Millions of pieces have been used to make the pictures, and if you will notice carefully you will see that they have the rough surface which catches the light as do all the early Venetian mosaics."

Giusippe nodded.

"There must also be some fine old glass windows in London," he speculated. "Aren't there, Mr. Cabot?"

"Yes, some varieties that you did not have in Venice, too," declared Uncle Bob. "You see other people did invent something, Giusippe. Here in England in some of the older houses there are windows made of tiny pieces of white glass leaded together; people were not able at that time to get large sheets of glass such as we now use, and I am not sure that these windows made of small leaded panes were not prettier. Then you will find other windows made from what we call bull's eye glass. These bull's eyes were the centers or waste from large discs of crown glass after all the big pieces possible had been cut away. As most glass comes now in sheets crown glass is little made, and therefore we find bull's eyes rare unless manufactured expressly to imitate the antique roundels."

"Of course there is lots of old stained glass in England, isn't there, Uncle Bob?" Jean ventured.

"Yes, indeed. I am sorry to say, however, that much of it has been destroyed before the public realized its value. At Salisbury Cathedral, for instance, some of the fine old glass was taken down and beaten to pieces in order that the lead might be used. At Oxford rare Gothic windows were removed and broken up to give room for the more modern work of the Renaissance. But you will still find at Canterbury and in many other of the English churches stained glass which has escaped destruction and come down to us through hundreds of years. And speaking of how such things have been preserved I must tell you the wonderful story of the east window in St. Margaret's Chapel at Westminster."

"Oh, do tell us!" begged Jean. "I love stories."

"This story is almost like a fairy tale, when one considers that it is the history of such a fragile thing as a glass window,"

Mr. Cabot began. "This window of which I am telling you was Flemish in design, and is said to have been ordered by Ferdinand and Isabella when their daughter Catherine was engaged to Arthur, the Prince of Wales. But for some reason it was not delivered, and a Dutch magistrate later decided to present it to King Henry the Seventh. Unfortunately the king died before the gift arrived and it came into the hands of the Abbot of Waltham. Now these were very troublous times for a stained glass window to be traveling about the land; Cromwell was in power and his followers believed it right to destroy everything which existed merely because of its beauty. So the old abbot was afraid his treasure would be wrecked, and to insure its safety he buried it."

"How funny!"

"Yes, wasn't it?"

"What happened then?"

"After the Restoration one of the loyal generals of the Crown had the window dug up and placed in a chapel on his estate. But the house changed hands and as its new owner did not like the window he offered it to Wadham College. The college authorities, alas, did not care for it, so it remained cased up for many years. Then by and by along came an Englishman who had the courage to buy it and have it set up in his house."

"Was that the end of it?" queried Giusippe.

"No, indeed. This person died, and his son took down the stained glass heirloom and in 1758 sold it to a committee which was at that time busy decorating St. Margaret's Chapel. Here at last it was set up and here one cannot but hope it will remain. Certainly it has earned a long rest."

"Shouldn't you think it would have been broken in all that time?" ejaculated Jean.

"One would certainly have thought so," Uncle Bob agreed. "It seemed to possess a charmed life. Most of that early glass was made by Flemish refugees who had fled to England to escape religious persecution. Some was designed for English monasteries. Houses, you know, did not have glass windows at that time but depended for protection upon oiled paper and skins. Glass was considered a luxury, and it was many, many years before window glass or table glass was in use. Rich English families bought glass dishes from galleys which, as Giusippe has told us, came laden from Venice. Sometimes this Venetian glass was mounted in gold or silver. There was, it is true, a little glass of English make, but no one thought it worth using; in fact when the stained glass windows were put into Beauchamp Chapel at Warwick it was expressly stated that no English glass was to be used."

"How did glass ever come to be made here, then?" inquired Jean.

"Well, in time more Flemish Protestants fled to England and began making stained glass at London, Stourbridge, and Newcastle-on-Tyne. In 1589 there were fifteen glass-houses in England. Then, because so much wood had been used in the iron foundries, the supply became exhausted and sea or pit coal had to be used instead. People were forced to try, in consequence, a different kind of melting pot for their glass and a new mixture of material; in this way they stumbled upon a heavy, brilliant, white crystal metal which the French called 'the most beautiful glassy substance known.' It was the pure white flint, or crystal glass, for which England has since become famous. Immediately it began to be used for all sorts of things. In 1637 the Duke of Buckingham had flint glass windows for his coach, and he had some Venetian workmen make mirrors out of it. So it went. A great many more mirrors were made, great pier glasses with beveled edges. It is said that some of those very mirrors are even now at Hampton Court. In the course of time the English became more and more skilful at glass-making, and when Queen Victoria came to the throne they were manufacturing enormous cut glass ornaments and bowls, and decorating their palaces and theaters with glass chandeliers which had myriads of heavy, sparkling prisms dangling from them. You will remember that in Venice you saw some glass chandeliers; and you may recall how delicately fashioned they were and how their twisted branches were covered with glass flowers in the center of which candles could be set. But the English chandeliers were far more massive affairs than those. And no sooner did English workmen find what they could do with this new material than they went mad over glass-making. Why, in 1851 they actually built for the first International Exhibit a Crystal Palace with a big glass fountain in it. Its builder was James Paxton, and he was knighted for doing it."

"I should think he deserved to be!" Jean said. "Who ever would have thought of making a palace of glass!"

"This one attracted much attention, I assure you," said Uncle Bob. "Later it was reconstructed at Sydenham and to this day there it stands. England now makes the finest crystal glass of any country in the world; but to-morrow I intend to take you to the British Museum and show you that in spite of all that European nations have done there were other very skilful glass-makers in the world before any of them made glass at all."

"Before the time of the Greeks and Romans—before the people who made the Naples Vase?" Jean asked.

"Yes, centuries before."

"Who were they?" demanded both Jean and Giusippe in the same breath.

"The Egyptians first; and after them the Phœnicians and Syrians. All these peoples lived where they could easily get plenty of the fine white sand necessary for glass-making. In some of the old tombs glass beads, cups, drinking-vessels, and curiously shaped vials have been found, many of them very beautiful in color. Some of this color is due to the action of the soil and the atmosphere, for science tells us that after glass has been buried in the earth many centuries and is then exposed to the air it begins to decay and its color often changes. We have in our museums many pieces of ancient glass which have changed color in this way and have become far more beautiful than they originally were. How these races that lived in the remote ages found out how to make glass no one knows; but certain it is that the Egyptians could fashion imitation gems, crude mosaics and various glass vessels. Later the Phœnicians improved the art and afterward, as you have seen, the Greeks and Romans took it up. There is a strange tale of how, during the reign of Tiberius, a glass-maker discovered how to make a kind of glass which would not break. It was a sort of malleable glass."

"Oh, tell us about it, please, Uncle Bob."

"Certainly, if you would like to hear. This glass-maker made a cup for the Emperor and tried a long time to get an audience at which to present his new invention. Then at last the chance came, and thinking to make himself famous the artisan contrived, as he passed the flagon to his sovereign, to drop it on the marble floor. Of course every one thought the glass was broken, and that is precisely what the glass-maker wanted them to think. He picked it up, smoothed out with his hammer the dent made in its side, and passed it once more expecting to receive praise for his wonderful deed. Tiberius eyed him silently. Then he asked; 'Does any one else know how to make glass like this?'

"'No one,' answered the glass-maker.

"'Off with his head at once!' cried the enraged monarch. 'If glass dishes and flasks do not break they will soon become as valuable as my gold and silver ones!'

"Despite his protests the poor glass-maker was dragged off and beheaded. The rulers of those days were not very fair-minded, you see."

With so many interesting stories, and so many things to see, you may be sure that neither Jean nor Giusippe found sightseeing dull. And the next day Uncle Bob was as good as his word, and took the young people to the British Museum, where he showed them some of the old Egyptian and Græco-Syrian glass. There were little vases, cups, and flasks of wonderful iridescent color, as well as many glass beads that had been found upon Egyptian mummies.

"Now, Uncle Bob," Jean said, after they had looked at these strange old bits of glass for some time, "you must take us to see the Portland Vase. You promised you would, you know."

"Sure enough; so I did. I should have forgotten it, too, had you not mentioned it."

Accordingly they hunted up the Gold Room where the vase stood.

Jean was very proud that she was able to point it out before she had been told which one it was.

"You see," explained she shyly, "it is so much like the Naples Vase that I recognized it right off."

It was indeed of the same dark blue transparent glass, and had on it the same sort of delicate white cameo figures.

"This vase," Mr. Cabot said, "was found about the middle of the sixteenth century enclosed in a marble sarcophagus in an underground chamber which was located two and a half miles out of Rome. It was taken to the Barbarini Palace, but later the princess of that noble family, wishing to raise money, sold it to Sir William Hamilton, who chanced to be at that time the English ambassador to Naples. From him it passed to the Duchess of Portland, and at her death was sold at auction to the new Duke of Portland. That is the way it got its name. Now the Duke, desirous of putting his precious purchase in a safe place, and also wishing to allow others to enjoy it, lent it to the British Museum. Imagine his horror and that of the Museum authorities when in 1845 a lunatic named Lloyd, who saw it, viciously smashed it to pieces."

His hearers gasped.

"To see it you would not dream that it had ever been broken, would you? Yes, it has been so carefully mended that no one could tell the difference. It was this vase which the English potter, Wedgwood, coveted so intensely that he bid a thousand pounds for it; the Duke of Portland outbid him by just twenty-nine pounds. He was, however, a generous man, and when at last the vase was his he allowed Wedgwood to copy it. This took a year's time, and even then the copy was far less beautiful than was the original. Many copies of it have been made since, but never has any one succeeded in making anything to equal the vase itself. You will see copies of it in almost all our American museums."

"I mean to see when I get home if there is a copy of it in Boston," Jean remarked.

"You will find one at the Art Museum. And now while we are here there is still that other famous vase which I mentioned once before and which I should like to have you see. It is not, perhaps, as fine as the Naples or the Portland, but it is nevertheless one celebrated the world over. Like the Naples Vase it came from Pompeii, and like the Portland Vase it has been skilfully mended. It is called the Auldjo Vase."

Uncle Bob was not long in finding where this treasure stood. It was small—not more than nine inches in height, and like the other two was of the familiar blue transparent glass with a white cameo design cut upon it. Instead of having a Grecian decoration, however, the pattern was of vines, leaves, and clusters of grapes.

"The Portland Vase, as I have already told you, was perfect when it was unearthed," Mr. Cabot said. "And the Naples Vase you will remember was also whole except that its base, or foot, which was probably of gold, was missing. But the Auldjo Vase was in pieces, and it was only a single one of these fragments that was bequeathed to the British Museum by Miss Auldjo. Now when the Museum committee saw this single piece nothing would do but they must have the others. They therefore bought the rest, had the vase mended, and set it up here where people can see it. It cost a great deal of money to purchase it."

"I think it is splendid of museums and of rich people to buy such things and put them where every one can look at them!" exclaimed Jean. "None of us could afford to and if those who owned them just kept them in their own houses we should never see them at all."

"Yes. Remember that, too, in this day when there are so many persons who begrudge the rich their fortunes. Remember if there were not individuals in the world who possessed fortunes the poor would have far less opportunity to see art treasures of every sort. And that is one way in which those who are rich and generous can serve their country. There are many different methods of being a good citizen, you see."

Mr. Cabot took out his watch and glanced at it thoughtfully.

"I think we shall have time to see just one thing more, and then we must go back to the hotel. We have examined all kinds of glass objects—so many, in fact, that it would seem as if there was no other purpose for which glass could be used. And yet I can show you something of which, I will wager, you have not thought."

"What is it?" questioned the two young people breathlessly.

Full of curiosity, Uncle Bob led them through several corridors until he came to a large room that they had not visited. He conducted them to its farther end and paused before a large sand glass.

"Before the days of clocks and watches," he began, "such glasses as these were much in use for telling the time. Throughout the sixteenth and seventeenth centuries they had them in almost all the churches, that the officiating clergyman might be able to measure the length of his sermon."

Jean laughed.

"I wish they had them now," she declared mischievously.

"Sometimes I do," smiled Uncle Bob. "It is said the glasses were originally invented in Egypt. Wherever they came from, they certainly were a great convenience to those who had no other means of telling the time. Charlemagne, I have read, had a sand glass so large that it needed to be turned only once in twelve hours. Fancy how large it must have been. At the South Kensington Museum is a set of four large sand glasses evidently made to go together. Of course you have seen, even in our day, hour, quarter-hour, and minute glasses."

"I used to practice by an hour glass," Jean replied quickly. "At least it was a quarter-of-an-hour glass, and I had to turn it four times."

"It would be strange not to have clocks and watches, wouldn't it?" reflected Giusippe as they walked back to the hotel.

"I guess it would!" Hannah returned emphatically. "The meals would never be on time."

"One advantage in that, my good Hannah, would be that nobody would ever be scolded because he was late," retorted Mr. Cabot humorously.

The three weeks allotted for the London visit passed only too quickly, and surprisingly soon came the day when the travelers found themselves aboard ship and homeward bound.

Perhaps after all they were not altogether sorry, for despite the marvels of the old world there is no place like home. Hannah was eager to open the Boston house and air it; Jean rejoiced that each throb of the engine brought her nearer to her beloved doggie; Uncle Bob's fingers itched to be setting in place the Italian marbles he had ordered for the new house;

and Giusippe waited almost with bated breath for his first sight of America, the country of his dreams.

But a great surprise was in store for every one of these persons as the mighty steamer left her moorings and put out of Liverpool harbor.

Across the deck came a vision, an apparition so unexpected that Jean and Giusippe cried out, and even Uncle Bob muttered to himself something which nobody could hear. The figure was that of a girl—a girl with wind-tossed hair who, with head thrown back, stopped a moment and looked full into the sunset.

It was Miss Ethel Cartright of New York, Giusippe's beautiful lady of Venice!

CHAPTER VII

AMERICA ONCE MORE

HE voyage from Liverpool to Boston was thoroughly interesting to Giusippe. In the first place there was the wonder of the great blue sea—a sea so vast that the Italian boy, who had never before ventured beyond the canals of the Adriatic, was bewildered when day after day the giant ship plowed onward and still, despite her speed, failed to reach the land. Sunlight flooded the water, twilight settled into darkness, and yet on every hand tossed that mighty expanse of waves. Would a haven ever be reached, the lad asked himself; and how, amid that pathless ocean, could the captain be so sure that eventually he would make the port for which he was aiming? It was all wonderful.

Fortunately the crossing was a smooth one, and accordingly every moment of the voyage was a delight. What happy days our travelers passed together! Miss Cartright was the jolliest of companions. She dressed dolls for Jean—dressed them in such gowns as never were seen, dainty French little

74

frocks which converted the plainest china creature into a wee Parisian; she read aloud; she told stories; she played games. Hannah surrendered unconditionally when, one morning after they had been comparing notes on housekeeping, the fact leaked out that Miss Cartright's mother had been a New Englander. That was enough!

"She has had the proper sort of bringing up," remarked Hannah, with a sigh of satisfaction. "She knows exactly how to pack away blankets and how to clean house as it should be done. She is a very unusual young woman!"

Coming from Hannah such praise was phenomenal.

Mr. Cabot seemed to think, too, that Miss Cartright possessed many virtues.

At any rate he enjoyed talking with her, and every evening when the full moon touched with iridescent beauty the wide, pulsing sea he would tuck the girl into her steamer chair and the two would stay up on deck until the clear golden ball of light had climbed high into the heaven.

So passed the voyage.

Then as America came nearer Giusippe witnessed all the strange sights that heralded the approach to the new continent; he saw the lights dotting the coast; he watched steamers which were outward bound for the old world he had left behind; he strained his eyes to catch, through a telescope, the murky outlines of the land.

"Here is still another use to which glass is put, Giusippe," said Mr. Cabot indicating with a gesture the red flash-light of a beacon far against the horizon. "Without the powerful reflectors, lenses, and prisms which are in use in our light-houses many a vessel would be wrecked. For not only must a lighthouse have a strong light; it must also have a means of throwing that light out, and thereby increasing its effectiveness. Scientists have discovered just how to arrange prisms, lenses, and reflectors so the light will travel to the farthest possible distance. At Navasink, on the highlands south of New York harbor, stands the most powerful coast light in the United States. It equals about sixty million candle-power, and its beam can be seen seventy nautical miles away. The carrying of the light to such a tremendous distance is due to the strong reflectors employed in conjunction with the light itself. The largest lens, however, under control of the United States is on the headlands of the Hawaiian Islands. This is eight and three-quarters feet in diameter and is made from the most carefully polished glass. And by the way, among other uses that science makes of glass are telescopes, microscopes, and field-glasses, which are all constructed from flawlessly ground lenses. Often it takes a whole year, and sometimes even longer, to polish a large telescope lens. Without this magnifying agency we should have no astronomy, and fewer scientific discoveries than we now have. The glasses people wear all have to be ground and polished in much the same fashion; opera glasses, magic lanterns, and every contrivance for bringing distant objects nearer or making them larger are dependent for their power upon glass lenses."

"Even when making glass I never dreamed it could be used for so many different purposes," answered Giusippe.

"I wish we had counted up, as we went along, how many things it is used for," Jean put in.

"We might have done so, only I am afraid you would have become very tired had we attempted it," laughed Uncle Bob. "In addition to optical glass there are still other branches of science that could not go on without glass in its various forms. Take, for instance, electricity. It would not be safe to employ this strange force without the protection of glass barriers to hedge in its dangerous current. Glass, as you probably know, is a non-conductor of electricity, and whenever we wish to confine its power and prevent it from doing harm we place a layer of glass between it and the thing to be protected. The glass checks the progress of the current. In all chemical laboratories, too, no end of glass test-tubes, thermometers, and crucibles are in demand for furthering research work. Science would be greatly hampered in its usefulness had it not recourse to glass in its manifold forms."

"What a wonderful material it is!" ejaculated Jean. "I never shall see anything made of glass again without thinking of all it does for us."

"Be grateful, too, Jean, to the men who have discovered how to use it," replied Mr. Cabot gravely. "Certainly our mariners many a time owe their safety to just such warning beacons as the one ahead. We must ask the captain what light that is. Just think—to-morrow morning we shall wake up in Boston harbor and be at home again."

A hush fell on the party.

"I shall be dreadfully sorry to have Miss Cartright leave us and go to New York; sha'n't you, Uncle Bob?" said Jean at last, slipping her hand into that of the older woman who stood beside her. "Wouldn't it be nice, Miss Cartright, if you lived in Boston? Then I'd see you all the time—at least I would when I wasn't in Pittsburgh, and then Uncle Bob could see you, and that would be almost as good."

"Almost," echoed Uncle Bob.

"But you are coming to New York to see me some time, Jean dear," the girl said with her eyes far on the horizon. "You know your uncle has promised that when you go to Pittsburgh both you and Giusippe are to stop and visit me for a few days."

"Yes, I have not forgotten; it will be lovely, too," replied Jean. "Still that is not like having you live where you can dress dolls all the time. Why don't you move to Boston? I am sure you would like it. We have the loveliest squirrels on the Common!"

Everybody laughed.

"I have been trying to tell Miss Cartright what a very nice place Boston is to live in," added Mr. Cabot softly.

"Well, we all will keep on telling her, and then maybe she'll be convinced," Jean declared.

So they parted for the night.

With the morning came the bustle and confusion of landing. Much of Uncle Bob's time was taken up with the inspection of trunks, and with helping Giusippe sign papers and answer the questions necessary for his admission to the United States. Then came the parting. They bade a hurried good-bye to Miss Cartright, whom Uncle Bob was to put aboard the New York train, and into a cab bundled Hannah, Giusippe, and Jean, in which equipage, almost smothered in luggage, they were rolled off to Beacon Hill.

Nothing could exceed Giusippe's interest in these first glimpses of the new country to which he had come. For the next few weeks he went about as if in a trance, struggling to adjust himself to life in an American city. How different it was from his beloved Venice! How sharp the September days with their early frost! How he missed the golden warmth of the sunny Adriatic and the familiar sights of home! During his journey through France and England the constant change of travel had carried with it sufficient excitement to keep him from being homesick; but now that he was settled for a time in Boston he got his first taste of what life in the United States was to be like. Not that he was disappointed; it was only that he felt such a stranger to all about him. The automobiles, subways, elevated roads, all confused his brain, and the dusty streets made his throat smart with dryness.

Daily, however, he became more and more accustomed to his surroundings, and when at last he ventured out alone and discovered that he could find his way back again his courage rose. Then he began going on errands for Hannah, and was proud and glad to be of use. He accompanied Uncle Bob to his office and arrived home alone in safety. Gradually the strangeness of his new home wore away. Every novel sight he beheld, every custom which was surprising to him, everything that he did not understand he asked a score of questions about. It was *why, why, why*, from morning until night. His questions, fortunately, were intelligent ones, and as he remembered with accuracy the answers given him and applied the knowledge thus gained to future conditions he made amazing headway in becoming Americanized. He got books and read them; he visited the churches, Library, and Art Museum. And when he saw how much of its beauty the New World had borrowed from the Old he no longer felt cut off from his Italian home.

Uncle Bob, in the meantime, had been forced to plunge so deeply into business that he had had little opportunity to aid his protégé in these explorations. But one Saturday noon he came home and announced that he was to treat himself to a half holiday.

"I am not going back to the office to-day," he declared. "Instead I intend to carry off you two young persons and show you something very beautiful, the like of which you will see nowhere else in all the world."

"What is it?" cried Jean and Giusippe.

"Oh, I'm not telling. Just you be ready directly after luncheon to go with me to Cambridge."

"Cambridge! Oh, I know. It is the University, Mr. Cabot. It is Harvard!" exclaimed Giusippe, very proud of his knowledge.

"Not quite," Mr. Cabot said, shaking his head, "although, being a Harvard man, I naturally feel that the equal of my Alma Mater cannot be found elsewhere. But you are on the right track. It is something which is out at Harvard. Guess again."

"I don't know," confessed Giusippe.

"Well, you may be excused because you have not been in this country long enough to be acquainted with all its marvels. But Jean should know. Where are you, young lady? You at least should be able to tell what treasures America possesses."

"I am afraid I can't."

"Then we must excuse you also; you are so young. I see plainly that we must appeal to Hannah. She who is ever extolling Boston can of course tell us what it is that Harvard University possesses which is unsurpassed in any other part of the world."

Hannah looked chagrined.

"You do not know?" went on Uncle Bob teasingly. "Oh, for shame! And you such an ardent Bostonian! Well, so far as I can see there is nothing for it but for me to take you all three to Cambridge as fast as ever we can get there. Such ignorance is deplorable."

You may be very sure that during the ride out from the city every means was employed to get Uncle Bob to tell what particular wonder he was to display. At last, driven to desperation by Jean's persistent questions, he answered:

"I will tell you just one fact. The things we are going to see are made of glass."

"Glass! But we have already seen everything that ever could be made from glass, Uncle Bob," cried Jean in dismay.

"No, we haven't."

"Is it stained glass windows?"

"No."

"Mosaics?"

"No."

"A telescope?"

"No."

"What is it, Uncle Bob?"

"Never you mind. You would never guess if you guessed a lifetime. You better give it up," was Mr. Cabot's smiling answer.

Cambridge was soon reached, and after a walk through the College Yard that Giusippe might have a peep at Holworthy, where Uncle Bob had spent his student days, the sightseers entered a quiet old brick building and were led by Mr. Cabot into a room where stood case after case of blooming flowers. There were garden blossoms of every variety, wild flowers, tropical plants, all fresh and green as if growing. And yet they were not growing; instead they lay singly or in clusters, each bloom as perfect as if just cut from the stalk.

"How beautiful! Oh, Uncle Bob, it is like a big greenhouse!" exclaimed Jean.

"This is what I brought you to see."

"But you said we were coming to see something made of glass," objected Giusippe.

"You did say so, Uncle Bob."

"Behold, even as I said!"

"Bu-u-t, these flowers are not glass. What do you mean?"

"On the contrary, my unbelieving friends, glass is precisely what they are made of. Every blossom, every leaf, every bud, every seed here is the work of an expert glass-maker."

Mr. Cabot watched their faces, enjoying their incredulity. *"Glass!"*

"Even so. Shall I tell you about it?"

"Yes! Yes!"

"This collection of flowers is called the Ware Collection, the name being bestowed out of compliment to Mrs. and Miss Ware, who generously donated much of the money for which to pay for it. Sometimes, too, it is known as the Blaschka Collection of Glass Flower Models, for the making was done by Leopold Blaschka and his son Rudolph, both of whom were Bohemians. It happened that several years ago Harvard University wished to equip its Botanical Department with flower specimens which might be used for study by the students. The question at once arose how this was to be done. Real flowers would of course fade, and wax flowers would melt or break. What could be used? There seemed to be no such thing as imperishable flowers."

Mr. Cabot paused a moment while the others waited expectantly.

"There were, however, in the Zoölogical Department some wonderfully accurate glass models of animals made by a Bohemian scientist named Blaschka, who was a rather remarkable combination of scholar and glass-maker. Accordingly when it became necessary to have fadeless flowers one of the professors wondered if this same Bohemian could not reproduce them. So he set out for Blaschka's home at Hosterwirtz, near Dresden, to see."

"Did he have to go way to Germany to find out?"

"Yes, because in the first place he did not know that Blaschka could make flowers at all; and if he could he was not certain that he could make them perfectly enough to render them satisfactory for such a purpose. So he traveled to Germany and found the house where lived the famous glass-maker; and it was while waiting alone in the parlor that he saw on a shelf a vase containing what seemed to be a very beautiful fresh orchid."

"It was made of glass!" Jean declared, leaping at the truth.

"Yes; and it was so perfect that the Harvard professor could hardly believe his eyes. At that moment the scientist entered. He confessed that he had made the flower for his wife; indeed, he had made many glass orchids—one collection of some sixty varieties which had been ordered by Prince Camille de Rohan, but which had later been destroyed when the Natural History Museum at Liège had been burned. Since then, Blaschka explained, he had given all his attention to making models of animals. He said that his son Rudolph helped him, and that they two alone knew how the work was done. It was their knowledge of zoology and of botany added to their skill at glass-making which enabled them to turn out such correct copies of real objects."

"Of course the Harvard professor was delighted," Jean ventured.

"Indeed he was! Before he left he won a promise from Blaschka and his son to send to Cambridge a few flowers to serve as specimens of what they could do. Now you may fancy the rage of the Harvard authorities when on the arrival of the cases of flowers they found that almost all of them had been broken to bits in the New York Custom House. There was, however, enough left of the consignment to give to the Cambridge professors the assurance that the two Bohemians were well equal to the task demanded of them. Those who saw the shattered blossoms were most enthusiastic, and Mrs. Ware and her daughter told the authorities to order a limited number as a gift to the University. This second lot came safely and were so beautiful that Harvard at once arranged that the two Blaschkas send over to America all the flowers they could make for the next ten years."

"My!"

"Yes, that seems a great many, doesn't it?" Mr. Cabot assented, nodding to Jean. "But after all, it was not so tremendous as it sounds. You see Harvard needed a copy of every American flower, plant, and fruit. The making of them would take a great deal of time. Of course unless the collection was complete it would be of little use to students. So the Blaschkas began their work, and for a few years averaged a hundred sets of flowers a year. Then the father died and Rudolph was left to finish the work alone. You remember I told you that in true mediæval fashion they had kept the secret of their art to themselves; as a consequence there now was no one to aid the son in his undertaking. Twice he came to our country to get copies of flowers from which to work, toiling bravely on in order to finish the task his father had begun. He said he considered it a sort of monument or memorial to the elder man's genius. There you have the story," concluded Mr. Cabot. "No other such collection exists anywhere else in the world. Even with a microscope it is impossible to distinguish between the real flower and the glass copy."

"How were they made?" Giusippe demanded. "Was the glass blown?"

"No; the flowers were modeled. That is all I can tell you. The brittle glass was in some way made plastic so it could be shaped by hand or by instruments. Some of the coloring was put on while the material was hot; some while it was cooling; and some after it was cold. It all depended upon the result desired. But one thing is evident—the Blaschkas worked very quickly and with marvelous scientific accuracy."

"It is simply wonderful," said Giusippe. "Even at Murano there is nothing to equal this."

"I thought you, who knew so much of glass-making, would appreciate what such a collection represents in knowledge, toil, and skill. Furthermore it is beautiful, and for that reason alone is well worth seeing," answered Mr. Cabot.

"It is wonderful!" repeated the Italian lad.

All the way home the young Venetian was peculiarly silent. His national pride had received a blow. Bohemia had surpassed Venice at its own trade, the art of glass-making!

CHAPTER VIII

JEAN THREATENS TO STEAL GIUSIPPE'S TRADE

T was the next morning while Mr. Cabot and Giusippe were still discussing the Blaschka glass flowers that the Italian lad remarked:

"I have wondered and wondered ever since we went out to Harvard how those fragile flower models were annealed without breaking. It must have been very difficult."

"What is annealing?" inquired Jean, holding at arm's length a doll's hat and straightening a feather at one side of it.

"Annealing? Why, the gradual cooling of the glass after it has been heated."

"What do they heat it for?"

"Don't you know how glass is made?" Giusippe asked in surprise.

Jean shook her head.

"No. How should I?"

"Why—but I thought every one knew that!"

"I don't see why. How could a girl know about the work you men do unless you take the trouble to tell her?" Jean dimpled. "All through Europe you and Uncle Bob have talked glass, glass, glass—nothing but glass, and as you both seemed to understand what you were talking about I did not like to interrupt and ask questions; but I had no more idea than the man in the moon what you meant sometimes."

"Do you mean to say you know nothing at all about the process of glass-making, Jean?" asked Mr. Cabot.

"Not a thing."

"Well, well, well! You have been a very patient little lady, that is all I can say. Giusippe and I have been both rude and remiss, haven't we, Giusippe? I thought of course you understood; and yet it is not at all strange that you did not. As you say, how could you? Why didn't you ask us, dear?"

"Oh, I didn't like to. I hate to seem stupid and be a bother."

"You are neither of those things, dear child. Is she, Giusippe?"

"I should say not."

"Well then, if it is all the same to you, I do wish somebody would tell me whether glass is dug up out of the earth or is made of things mixed together like a pudding," said Jean.

Both Giusippe and Uncle Bob laughed.

"The pudding idea is the nearer correct. Glass is made from ingredients which are mixed together, boiled, baked, and set away to cool. Isn't that about it, Giusippe?"

Giusippe nodded.

"I think the best remedy we can administer to this young lady, as well as the most fitting penance for our own discourtesy to her, is to escort her through a glass factory and let her, with her own eyes, behold the process. What do you say, Giusippe?"

"A capital idea, señor. Then I, too, should have the chance to visit an American factory and compare the process you use here with our Italian method. I should like it above everything else."

"That is precisely what we will do then," declared Mr. Cabot. "On my first leisure day we will go, and in the meantime I will hunt up the location of the most satisfactory and nearest glass works."

Not more than a week passed before Uncle Bob fulfilled his promise.

"Make yourselves ready, oh ye glass-makers," said he one morning at breakfast. "I find after telephoning to the office that I am not needed to-day; therefore, the moment we have swallowed these estimable griddle cakes of Hannah's we will hie us forth to instruct Jean in the art of manufacturing vases, bottles, tumblers and the various sorts of glassware."

The two young people greeted the suggestion with pleasure.

"Can you really get away to-day, Uncle Bob?" cried Jean. "What fun we'll have!"

"I think it will be fun. We must, however, make Giusippe captain of the expedition for he is the one who really knows glass-making from beginning to end, and can answer all our questions."

"I think I might in Murano," returned the Venetian modestly, "but that is no sign that I can do it here; your process may differ from the one we use at home."

"Oh, I do not believe so—at least, not in essentials," Mr. Cabot answered.

So they started out, and before they had proceeded any distance at all they got into a spirited debate over the tiny lights of glass set in the top of the electric car. The panes were of ground glass dotted with an all-over pattern of small stars which had been left transparent.

"How did they make the stars on that glass?" was Jean's innocent question. "Did they scratch off the thick surface and leave the design of clear glass?"

"No indeed," Mr. Cabot replied. "On the contrary they started with the stars and then made the background cloudy."

"But I don't see how they could."

"Do you, Giusippe?"

"I am afraid not, señor."

"Good! At last there is one fact about glass-making that I can impart to you. This sort of glass is known as sand-blast glass, and the art of making it, they say, chanced to be discovered near the seashore. It was found that when the strong winds rose and blew the sand against glass window-panes of the houses the small particles, being sharp, cut into the glass surface, and before long wore it to a cloudy white through which it was impossible to see out. Often the glass fronts of lighthouses were injured in this way and the lights dimmed. Finally some man came along who said: 'See here! Why not turn this grinding effect of the sand to some purpose? Why not apply it to transparent glass and make it frosted so one can get light but not see through it? Often such glass would be a convenience.' Therefore this inventor set his brain to the task. Strong currents or streams of sand were directed against a clear glass surface with such force that they cut and ground it until it was no longer transparent. They called the product thus made sand-blast glass. Later they improved upon it by laying a stencil over it so that a desired design was covered and remained protected from the sand blast. The result was a pattern such as you see—clear figures set in a background of clouded glass."

"How interesting!"

"Yes, isn't it? As is true of so many other of our most clever inventions nature first showed man the path. Ground glass in its modified forms is used for many purposes now; and yet I venture to say few persons know how it came to be discovered."

Just at this point the car stopped with a sudden jerk, and beckoning Jean and Giusippe to follow, Mr. Cabot got out and entered a large brick building that stood close at hand. Evidently he was expected, for a man came forward to greet him.

"Mr. Cabot?" he asked.

"Yes. I received your note this morning, so I brought my young charges out at once. It is very good of you to allow us to go through the factory."

"We are always glad to see visitors. I will put you in the hands of one of our foremen who will take you about and tell you everything you may want to know."

He touched a bell.

"Show Mr. Cabot and his friends down-stairs," said he to the boy who answered his call, "and introduce them to Mr. Wyman. Tell him he is to conduct them over the works."

Mr. Wyman welcomed them cordially.

"We see many visitors here, sir," said he, "and are always glad to have them come. Although glass-making is an old story to us scarce a day passes that some one does not visit us to whom the process is entirely new; and it certainly is interesting if a person has never seen it. Suppose we begin at the very beginning. In this bin, or trough, you will see the mixture or batch of which the glass is made. It is composed of red lead and the finest of white beach sand. The lead is what gives the inside of the trough its vermilion color. The sand comes from abroad, and before it can be used it must be sifted and sifted through a series of closely woven cloths until it is smooth and fine as powder. Before we put the mixture into the melting pots we heat it to a given temperature so that it will be less likely to chill the clay pots and break them."

"Do you really make glass by melting up that stuff?" asked Jean incredulously.

The man smiled.

"But isn't it all red?"

"The red comes out in the melting. We have to be very careful, however, in weighing out the ingredients, for much of our success depends on the accurate proportions of the materials combined in the batch. Of course the chemical composition differs some for different sorts of glass. It all depends on what kind of glass is to be made. Then too the conditions of the furnaces vary at times, the draughts being better at some seasons than at others. We take a test or proof of every fresh melt, and you would be surprised to see how little these differ. Careful mixing of the raw materials is the first important item of successful glass-making; the second is the fusion by heat of the materials."

"The batch is next melted, Jean," explained Giusippe, as

they followed Mr. Wyman into the great brick-paved room where the furnaces were.

Here indeed was a picturesque scene. Numberless men were hurrying hither and thither, some whirling in the air glowing masses of molten glass; others standing before the furnace doors gathering balls of it on the end of long iron blow-pipes which were from six to nine feet in length. Everybody was scurrying. As soon as a ball of red-hot glass had been collected on the end of a blow-pipe it was rushed off to the blower before it cooled. In and out of the throng of moving workmen young boys, or carriers, swung along bearing to the annealing ovens on charred wooden trays or forks newly completed vases or pitchers.

Jean glanced about, fascinated by the bustling crowd.

"Here are the furnaces," the foreman said. "Each one has twelve openings and is built with a low dome to keep in the heat. The flues or chimneys are in the sides of the furnace. Within, and just beneath the openings or working-holes, stand the great clay pots of molten batch. These pots are made for us from New Jersey clay; formerly we used to make them ourselves, but it was a great deal of trouble, and we now find it simpler to buy them. They vary in cost from thirty to seventy-five dollars, according to their size."

"And they are liable to break the first time they are used," whispered Giusippe in a jesting undertone.

Mr. Wyman caught his words.

"Ah, you know something of glass-making then, my young man?"

"A little."

"The pots are, as you say, a great lottery. Sometimes one

will be in constant use three months or longer, and do good service; on the other hand a pot may break the first time using and let all the melt into the furnace. Then we have a lively time, I can tell you, ladling it out, and taking care in the meantime that none of the other pots are upset."

Giusippe nodded appreciatively.

Many a day just such a catastrophe had occurred when he had been working; vividly he recalled how all the men had been forced to come to the rescue.

"Are the pots filled to the top with batch?" asked Mr. Cabot.

"Yes, we charge them pretty solid; but the raw material loses bulk in melting, so they have to be filled in as the melt settles. At the end of ten or twelve hours we have a refilling or *topping out*, as we call it; usually this is enough. The first fill must become fluid and its gases must escape before any more material is added; we also have to be sure when we put the pots in the furnace that the temperature is high enough to melt the batch immediately, or the glass will go bad."

"What do you use for fuel?"

"Crude oil. In the West they can get natural gas, and there they often melt the batch in tanks instead of pots. But we find crude oil quite satisfactory. You can readily understand that we cannot burn any fuel that gives off a waste product such as coal dust or cinders, because if we did such matter would get into the melt and speck the glass, causing it to be imperfect. Much of the work done by the earliest glass-makers was specked in this way, and in fact the genuineness of old glass is sometimes determined from these very imperfections."

"I see," Mr. Cabot nodded.

"After the melt is in a fluid state it throws to the top, provided the heat is sufficient, many impurities such as bubbles and scum. These are, of course, skimmed off—a process called plaining. Afterward the hot material has to be cooled before it can be worked, and reduced from fluid to a thicker consistency. This we call *standing off* or *fining*."

"How long does it take to melt the batch and get it ready to use?"

"About three days. We run a relay of furnaces—three of them—and plan so that a melt will be ready to be worked every other day; in that way we keep plenty of usable material on hand."

"And then?"

"Then we are ready to go ahead and blow it. We make nothing but the better grades of blown glass here; that is, no window glass or cheap pressed ware. Of course there are some patterns, such as fluted designs and their like, which cannot be entirely fashioned by the blower; therefore these are first blown as nearly the required size as possible and are then made into the desired form by shutting them inside iron moulds and squeezing them into the proper shape. You shall see it done later on."

He now led them up to where a gatherer stood at one of the working-holes of the furnace.

"This man," explained Mr. Wyman, "is collecting on his blow-pipe enough glass to make a pitcher. He uses his judgment as to the amount necessary, but so often has he estimated it that he seldom gets either too much or too little. He will next carry it to the blower, who will blow it into a long, pear-shaped cylinder the size he wants the pitcher to be."

They followed, and with much interest watched a great

Swede fill his lungs and blow into the smaller end of the iron pipe with all his strength; immediately the ball of soft, red-hot glass began to take form. With incredible speed the blower flattened its base upon a marver or table topped with sheet iron. A short iron rod or pontil was next fastened to the middle of the bottom of the pitcher in order that the blower might hold it, and after this had been done the blow-pipe was detached. The glass-maker sat in a sort of backless chair which had long, flat, metal-covered arms at either side, and as he worked he rolled the rod with its plastic material back and forth along one of these iron arms to shape it. He then took his shears and, making an incision at the middle of the back of the jug, he began to cut the top into the shape he wanted it, depending entirely on his eye for the outline. Then quick as a flash he seized a bit of round metal not unlike a beet in shape and, pressing it inside the soft glass, made the depression for the nose. All this was done in much less time than it takes to tell it. A small boy, or carrier, now bobbed up at just the proper moment and taking the pitcher on his wooden fork carried it off to a small furnace where it was reheated at the opening or "glory hole." This little furnace, Mr. Wyman said, was used only for the purpose of softening glass objects which became chilled in the modeling and began to be hard and less pliable. As soon as the boy brought the pitcher back another lad, as if calculating by magic the precise moment at which to appear, approached with a small mass of molten glass at the end of his gathering-iron. This he stuck firmly against the pitcher at the correct spot to form the base of the handle; the modeler snipped off with his shears as much of the soft glass as he thought necessary, turned it up, and in the twinkling of an eye fastened the upper end of the handle in place. Then he surveyed his handiwork an instant to make sure that it was symmetrical, straightened it just a shade with his battledore of charred wood, and passed it over to the carrier, who bore it off to be baked.

"Why do they use so much charred wood for the shaping?" inquired Jean.

"Metal things are liable to mark the glass, leaving upon it a print, scratch, or other imperfection; charred wood, when worn down, is absolutely smooth and cannot mar the material."

"Oh, yes, I see. And where have they taken the pitcher now?"

"We will follow it," replied the foreman.

Escorting them across the room he showed them a low oven or kiln. The door of it was open, and inside they could see all sorts of glassware which had just been finished.

"Here is where your pitcher will remain for the next three days," said he. "We build a fire, put the completed glass in the oven, and leave it there until the fire goes out and the oven gradually cools; we call the process annealing. It prevents the glass from breaking when exposed to friction or to the atmosphere. Glass is very brittle, and extremely sensitive to heat and cold. If it were not annealed it would not be strong, and would snap to pieces the moment it came in contact with the outer air. Now it is very difficult to anneal glass, the trouble being that all hollow ware is one temperature on the inside and another on the outside. Hence, when heated, the inside takes longer to cool. Any current of cold air that strikes it will fracture it. So, as you can readily see, an annealing kiln or oven must be arranged in such a way that it will allow the two surfaces to cool simultaneously."

"I think I understand," answered Jean. "And you say these things must stay in the kiln about three days?"

"Yes, the kiln takes about that time. It is a slow process, because we have practically no way of regulating its heat. A lehr does the work much quicker. Over here you will see one. It is a long arch or oven open at both ends. The glassware travels in iron pans along a moving surface from the hot oven, or receiving end, to the cool, or discharging end. The temperature of the lehr can be scientifically tested and regulated, and this is very necessary, because the heavy glass intended for cutting can stand a greater heat than can ordinary hollow ware such as vials and table glass. We regulate the oven according to what we are annealing in it. It does not take so long to anneal glass in a lehr as in a kiln, and therefore in many factories only lehrs are used. If you will come around to the cool end you can see some of the finished pieces being taken out. Each object is made by a certain set or gang of workmen—a shop, we call it. The work of each shop when taken from the lehr is put in a box by itself and is then counted up, and the men paid according to the number of perfect objects finished. It is piece work. For instance, one shop makes only pitchers, another wine-glasses, another vases, and so on. Every group has its specialty, and each workman in the team understands exactly what his part is in the whole. The common interest of turning out as many perfect pieces as possible spurs each man to work as rapidly, well, and helpfully as he can."

"Just like a football squad, Uncle Bob," laughed Jean.

"Exactly," nodded Mr. Wyman. "After the finished glass is taken from the kiln or lehr it goes to the examining room,

"IT IS SHAPED TO THE FORM REQUIRED"

where girls dip it in clear water and hold it to the light to test it for imperfections; then it is sorted, packed, and shipped."

"And vases, sugar-bowls, tumblers, and most of the hollow glassware is made in the same way?" inquired Mr. Cabot.

"Yes, practically so. The general scheme is the same. As I told you, there are some difficult designs which must be squeezed into shape in moulds. These are of iron, and for the convenience of the blowers are set in holes in the floor. They are made in two parts joined by a hinge. The molten glass is blown to the approximate size and then a boy shuts it inside the mould and the blower blows into it until it has entirely filled out the mould in which it is confined. When released it is shaped to the form required."

"But doesn't it stick to the mould?"

"Seldom. The moulds are painted over on the inside with a preparation which prevents the glass from sticking."

"Do you cut any glass here?"

"Oh, yes. Cut glass is made from the heavier crystal variety. The design is roughly outlined upon it in white and then the cutter places the part to be cut against an emery-wheel, which grinds out the grooves and figures and makes the pattern. Just above each cutter's revolving wheel is suspended a funnel of wet sand, and this drops at intervals upon the turning disc and cools it; otherwise it would become so hot from the friction that it could not be used. After the design has been cut on the emery-wheel all its rough edges are smoothed off on a stone of much finer grain. I can show you our glass cutters at work if you would care to see them."

"Oh, do let's see them, Uncle Bob," begged Jean.

"All right; but only for a few moments. We have already

taken too much of Mr. Wyman's time, I fear. And besides, I must be back in town for luncheon," answered Mr. Cabot.

Accordingly they went on into the next room, where Jean became so fascinated by the whirring wheels and the men whose steady hands guided them that it was with difficulty she could be persuaded to leave and start for home.

"Do you think, little lady, that when you get back to Boston you can mix up some glass for us and bake it in Hannah's oven?" questioned Uncle Bob of her when they were at last in the car.

"I am not sure," replied the girl with a bright smile. "But certainly I have a much clearer idea how to do it than I had before I went out to the factory. In future when you and Giusippe talk glass-making I can at least be a bit more intelligent. I think, too, I appreciate now how wonderful it was that the Egyptians, Persians, and Syrians discovered in those far-off days how to make glass. I am not at all sure, Giusippe, that when we go to Pittsburgh I shall not steal your trade and apply to Uncle Tom for a place in his factory."

Mr. Cabot pinched her cheek playfully.

"I guess you'd better stick to dressing dolls," he said.

CHAPTER IX

A REUNION

T length all too soon for Uncle Bob and Hannah, and indeed far sooner than Jean and Giusippe had realized, October came, and the time for starting for Pittsburgh was at hand. To the young people their departure was not without its anticipations. Jean longed to see Beacon and Uncle Tom, and Giusippe burned with eagerness to take up the position his uncle had secured for him at Mr. Curtis's factory.

"How odd it is, Giusippe," Jean mused one day, "that we each have an uncle waiting for us. And besides that you have an aunt, too, haven't you? I wish I had. I'd love to have an aunt! As it is I have only Beacon."

"Maybe you'll have one some day," was Giusippe's vaguely consoling answer. "But anyway I shouldn't think you would care much. You have Miss Cartright, and she is almost as good as an aunt."

"I suppose she is something like one," admitted Jean, "only, you see, she doesn't live where I do, so I can't see her very often. Of course she has sent me nice letters since she got home to New York and sometimes she writes Uncle Bob, too; but it isn't really like seeing her. When I think that the day after to-morrow she is to meet us in New York it seems too good to be true. Won't it be fun? I love Miss Cartright! Do you suppose she looks just the same as she did when she was with us on the steamer?"

"I suppose so. Your uncle said she did when he saw her in New York."

"I know it. He has had lots of chances to see her because he has been over there so many times on business trips. I wish we had. But we shall see her now, anyway. Oh, I am so glad!" Jean whirled enthusiastically round the room. "I think we are to have a pretty nice visit in New York if we do all the things Uncle Bob is planning to. He says he is going to take us to the studio of one of his friends and show us how stained glass windows are made. I shall like to see that, sha'n't you?"

So the boy and girl chattered on little dreaming, in the delight of the pleasures in store for them, how lonely at heart were Mr. Cabot and poor Hannah.

"If it wasn't that Jean is coming back in the spring I should be completely inconsolable," lamented Hannah. "I cannot bear to part with the child. But she will surely be back again, won't she, Mr. Bob? There won't be any other plan made? You'll certainly insist that Mr. Curtis send her home to us in May, won't you?"

"There, there, Hannah, dry your eyes. Of course Jean will be back. I have no more mind to lose her than you have.

No one knows how I love that child! I'd no more let her leave my home than I would cut off my right hand," was Mr. Cabot's vehement reply.

"The boy is a splendid fellow, too," Hannah went on. "He has the makings of a fine man, Mr. Bob."

"Yes. Giusippe is a very unusual lad. As time goes on I am more and more convinced that we made no mistake in bringing him to America. I am sure that we are adding a good citizen to the country. I have a feeling that Mr. Curtis will be much interested in him."

"I wish he'd be sufficiently interested to adopt him and send Jean home to us," suggested Hannah, smoothing out the edge of an apron she was hemming.

"I am afraid such a scheme as that would be too good to be true," laughed Mr. Cabot. "If, however, he helps place Giusippe in a fine business position I shall be satisfied. That is all I shall ask."

Nevertheless, brave as Uncle Bob tried to be, he was very solemn the morning he saw the trunks brought down-stairs and strapped on the back of the waiting cab.

"Cheer up, Hannah!" he called from the sidewalk. "Why, bless my soul, if you're not crying! Come, come, this will never do! May will be here before you know it, and the child will be back again. She is only going on a visit—remember that. Her home is here. Say good-bye to Hannah, you young scamps. She somehow seems to have the notion you are never to return. Tell her she is not to get off so easily. Before many moons she will find you two in the pantry raiding the cookie jar just as you robbed it yesterday—you bandits!"

And so with a gaiety he did not feel Mr. Cabot hustled his charges into the carriage and slammed the door.

The trip to New York was a blur of new impressions and the city itself, when they reached it, another blur—a confusion of madly rushing throngs; giant sky-scrapers; racing taxicabs; and clanging bells. To the children it seemed a maelstrom of horror. Their one thought was to get safely out of the crowd, have something to eat, and go to bed. But with the morning light New York took on quite a different aspect. It proved to be not such a bad place after all. The solitary fact that it harbored Miss Cartright was quite enough to redeem it in their eyes. Then there was so much to see which was new and strange! Directly after breakfast Uncle Bob took them out for a stroll and after a walk in the brisk air he led them into Tiffany's.

"While we have time and are right here I want to show you one of the most wonderful glass products of America," said he. "It is called Favril glass and is made at Coronna, Long Island. Just how, I do not know. The process is a secret one. You remember, don't you, the marvelous iridescent colors of the ancient Egyptian glass we saw in the British Museum? And you recall how exquisite was the turquoise glaze on some of the old pieces? Well, the Tiffany people have tried to imitate that, and so well have they succeeded that they have received many medals in recognition of their skill. Museums all over the world from Tokyo to Oslo have purchased collections of the glass that it may be exhibited and enjoyed by young and old. I am going to show you some of it now."

Up in an elevator they sped, and alighting at one of the upper floors Uncle Bob led the way into a room rich with silken hangings and rare oriental rugs; all about this room were vases, plates, lamp-shades, and ornaments of beautiful hues. There were great golden glass bowls glinting with elusive lights of violet, blue, and yellow; there were vases opalescent with burning flecks of orange and copper; there were green glass plates and globes which shaded into tones of blue as delicate as mother-of-pearl.

"Oh!" sighed Jean rapturously, "I never saw anything so lovely! Look at these plates, Uncle Bob, do look at them. How ever did they get the color? It is like a sunset."

"The Tiffanys, like Blaschka the flower modeler, are not telling the world how they get their results. Rest assured, however, many and many hours must have been spent in experiments before such artistic products could be obtained."

"Think of the struggles with color and with firing," Giusippe murmured.

"And the pieces that must have been spoiled!" put in Jean.

"But think of the triumph of at last taking from the lehrs such gems as these! The results which air, soil, and age have by chance produced in the ancient Egyptian and Græco-Syrian glass the Tiffanys have created in a modern ware. It is a great achievement, and a royal contribution to the art of the world."

The children would have been glad to linger for a much longer time in the vast shop had not the chime of a clock warned them that the noon hour, when they were to meet Miss Cartright, was approaching. She had promised to lunch with them all at the Holland House.

Yes, she looked just the same, "only prettier," Jean whispered to Giusippe. Certainly there was an added glow of beauty on her cheek and a new sweetness in her smile. How glad she was to see them! And how glad, glad, glad they were to see her. Miraculously from somewhere Uncle Bob produced a great bunch of violets which she fastened in her gown and then amid a confusion of merry chatter and laughter they went in to luncheon.

It was indeed a royal luncheon!

Uncle Bob seemed inclined to order everything on the menu, and it was not until Miss Cartright protested that not only the young people but she herself would be ill, that he was to be stayed. And what a joke it was when the waiter bent down and asked her if both her son and daughter would take some of the hot chocolate!

Oh, it was a jolly luncheon!

And after it was finished and they all had declared that not until next Thanksgiving could they think of eating anything more, off they shot in a taxicab to the studio of Uncle Bob's friend, Mr. Norcross, who had promised over the telephone to show them the window he was making for a church in Chicago.

They found the studio at the top of one of New York's high buildings, and it was flooded with light from the west and south; on one side of the room was an open space large enough to allow an immense stained glass window to be set up.

Mr. Norcross, who was an old college friend of Uncle Bob's, greeted them cordially and when Miss Cartright remarked on the airiness of his workshop he answered:

"Yes, I have plenty of air up here; of course I enjoy it, too. But air, after all, is not the important factor which I consider. My stock in trade is light. Without it I could do nothing. Through the medium of strong sunlight I must test my work, for stained glass is beautiful chiefly as the light plays through it. It is not a tapestry nor a picture—it is primarily a window. Its colors must be rich in the light but not glaring; and its design must be so thoughtfully executed that the telling figures will stand forth when there is a strong sunset, for instance, behind them."

"Of course, then, you must take care that the colors you use do not prove too powerful and overshadow your central figures," said Miss Cartright.

"Ah, you paint?"

"Yes, but not as I want to," was the wistful answer. "I do portraits. So I can readily see that your problem is a unique, and far more difficult one than mine. I have only a changeless color scheme to consider, while your colors shift with every cloud that passes across the sky."

Mr. Norcross nodded with pleasure at her instant appreciation of his difficulties.

"Have you ever seen stained glass in the making?" he asked.

She shook her head.

"Neither have any of the rest of us, Norcross," put in Mr. Cabot. "That is what we came for. I have been toting these two youthful friends of mine all over the world and together we have investigated almost every known form of glass, from the Naples Vase down to an American lamp chimney."

Mr. Norcross smiled.

"So you see," Uncle Bob went on, "I wanted them to witness this phase of glass-making."

"They certainly shall. How did you chance to be so interested in the making of glass?" inquired the artist, turning to Giusippe.

"I am a Venetian, señor. For over six generations my people have been at Murano."

"Oh, then, what wonder! And that accounts for your own personal color scheme."

The artist let his eyes dwell upon the Italian's face intently: then glanced at Miss Cartright.

"I did a portrait of Giusippe," she responded quietly, "when I was in Venice a few years ago. He did not look so much like an American then."

"Modern clothing certainly does take the picturesqueness out of some of us," answered Mr. Cabot.

In the meantime Giusippe had wandered off to the distant side of the studio and now stood before a large glass panel calling excitedly:

"Is this the window you are making, señor? How beautiful! The violet light behind the woman's head, and that yellow glow on her hair—it is wonderful! And her white drapery against the background of green!"

Mr. Norcross came to his side, flushing with gratification.

"The mellow tones playing on her hair were hard to get. I spent a lot of time working at them. It isn't easy to get the results one wants when making stained glass."

"What did you do first, Mr. Norcross, when you began the window?" asked Jean timidly.

"I will show you every step I have taken in doing it if you would like to follow the process. In the first place I went to Chicago and studied the light and the setting which it was to have. Then I made this small water-color design and submitted it for approval to the persons who were ordering the window. The drawing accepted, I set about making a full-sized cartoon which I sketched in with charcoal on this heavy paper; the black lines represent the leading and the horizontal stay-bars necessary to hold the glass in place. After that I sliced up my cartoon into a multitude of small pieces from which the glass could be cut and the lead lines decided upon. All this done I went to work planning my color scheme—thinking out what dominating colors I would use and where I would place my high lights."

"And then you were ready for your glass?" inquired Mr. Cabot.

"Yes. Now selecting the glass is not alone a matter of color; it is also a problem of thickness. Sometimes a variation in tone can be obtained merely by using a bit of heavier glass in some one spot. Again the effect must be obtained by the use of paint."

"What kind of glass do you use, Mr. Norcross?" Giusippe questioned.

"What we call bottle, or Norman, glass. We get it from England, and strangely enough there is a heavy duty on it in its raw state. One can import a whole window free of duty because it is listed as an art work; but the glass out of which an art work is to be constructed costs a very high price. Odd, isn't it? As soon as I reach the point of using glass I arrange it on a large plate glass easel, using wax in the spaces where the lead is to go. Then I experiment and experiment with my colors. You probably know that in making modern stained glass a great deal of paint is used in order to get shading and degrees of color. It was toward the end of the thirteenth century that the old glass-makers began to introduce the use of paint into their windows. First came the grisaille glass, as it was called, where instead of strong reds and blues most of the window was in white painted with scroll work in which a few bits of brilliant stained glass were set like jewels. Then with the fourteenth century came those elaborate painted canopies and borders within which were the main figures of the window in stained glass. From that time on the combination of stained and painted glass was used. Accordingly we all work by that method now. So, as I say, I paint in my glass and afterward it has to be fired, all the small pieces being laid out on heavy sheets of steel covered with plaster of paris."

"Do your colors always come out as you mean to have them?" inquired Giusippe, his eyes on the artist's face.

Mr. Norcross shrugged his shoulders.

"You know, don't you, how the firing often changes the tone, and how you frequently get a color you neither intended nor desired. That is one of the tribulations of stained glass making. Another is when the cutters must trim down the glass and put the lead in place. You may not realize that there are three widths of lead from which to select; it is not always easy to choose for every part of the design the thickness which will look the best. For instance, sometimes the leading will be too strong and overwhelm the picture; again it will be too weak and render the window characterless."

"It must be a fascinating puzzle to work out," mused Miss Cartright.

"Yes; but it is also a great test of the patience."

"Were the old glass windows made in this same way, do you suppose?" asked Jean after a pause.

"I presume the old glass-makers worked along the same general plan, although they may not have followed exactly the present-day methods; certain it is, however, that they knew all the many tricks or devices for getting color effects—knew them far better than we do now. And they put endless time and thought into their work, no artist feeling it beneath his dignity to follow the humblest detail of his conception. He watched over his art-child until it got to be full-grown. This is the only way to get fine results. For, you see, there is no set rule for a glass designer to apply. Each window presents a fresh problem in the management of light and color. There is no branch of art more elusive or more difficult than this. I must be able to construct a window which will be satisfactory as a flat piece of decoration; it must be sufficiently interesting to give pleasure even when it stands in a dim light. Then presto—the sun moves round, and my window is transformed! And in the flood of light that passes through it I must still be able to find it beautiful."

"I think that I should like to learn to make stained glass," declared Giusippe, who had become so absorbed that he had moved close beside Mr. Norcross.

"Would you?"

The artist smiled down kindly at him. "In your country you have many a fine example of glass. France, too, is rich in rose windows which are the despair of our modern craftsmen. But we glass-makers are working hard and earnestly, and who knows but in time we may give to the world such glass as is at Rheims, Tours, Amiens, and Chartres."

"What sort of paint do you use?" asked Mr. Cabot as he took up a brush and idly examined it in his fingers.

"A kind of opaque enamel containing fusible material which is melted by heat and thereafter adheres to the surface of the glass. It must, however, be used carefully, as it possesses so much body that too much of it will obscure the light—the thing a stained glass window should never do. We should have many more successful windows if the people making them would only bear in mind that a window is not a picture, and should not be treated as one. For my part, I make my window a window. I join the pieces of glass frankly together, not trying to conceal the lead that holds them. I cannot say that I get the results either with colors or lights that I want to get; but I am trying, with the old masters as my ideal."

"Certainly you are a long way on the road if you can turn out a window as beautiful as this one promises to be. None of us reaches the ideal, Mr. Norcross, but in the past is the inspiration that what man has done man can do. Perhaps not now, but in the future," Miss Cartright said softly.

"I wish I might try stained glass making," Giusippe said again.

"Perhaps some time you will, my boy," answered Mr. Norcross, "and perhaps, too, your generation may succeed where mine has failed, and give to the world another Renaissance. Remember, all the great deeds haven't been done yet."

CHAPTER X

TWO UNCLES AND A NEW HOME

NCLE TOM CURTIS arrived in New York toward the end of the children's visit, good-byes were said to Miss Cartright and to Uncle Bob, and within the space of a day Jean and Giusippe were amid new surroundings. Here was quite a different type of city from Boston—a city with many beautiful buildings, fine residences, and a swarm of great factories which belched black smoke up into the blue of the sky. Here, too, were Giusippe's aunt and uncle with a hearty welcome for him; and here, furthermore, was the new position which the boy had so eagerly craved in the glass works. The place given Giusippe, however, did not prove to be the one his uncle had secured for him after all; for during the journey from New York Uncle Tom Curtis had had an opportunity to study the young Italian, and the result of this better acquaintance turned out to be exactly what Uncle Bob Cabot had predicted; Uncle Tom became tremendously interested in the Venetian, and before they arrived at Pittsburgh

113

had decided to put him in quite a different part of the works from that which he had at first intended.

"Your nephew has splendid stuff in him," explained Mr. Curtis to Giusippe's uncle. "I mean to start him further up the ladder than most of the boys who come here. We will give him every chance to rise and we'll see what use he makes of the opportunity. He is a very interesting lad."

Accordingly, while Jean struggled with French, algebra, drawing, history, and literature at the new school in which Uncle Tom had entered her and while she and Fräulein Decker had many a combat with German, Giusippe began wrestling with the problems of plate glass making.

The factory was an immense one, covering a vast area in the manufacturing district of the city; it was a long way from the residential section where Jean lived, and as the boy and girl had become great chums they at first missed each other very much. Soon, however, the rush of work filled in the gaps of loneliness. Each was far too busy to lament the other, and since Uncle Tom invented all sorts of attractive plans whereby they could be together on Saturday afternoons and Sundays the weeks flew swiftly along. There were motor trips, visits to the museums and churches of the city, and long walks with Beacon wriggling to escape from the leash which reined him in.

Uncle Tom's home was much more formal than Uncle Bob's. It stood, one of a row of tall gray stone houses, fronting a broad avenue on which there was a great deal of driving. It had a large library and a still larger dining-room in which Jean playfully protested she knew she should get lost. But stately as the dwelling was it was not so big and formidable after all if once you got upstairs; on the second floor were Uncle Tom's rooms and a dainty little bedroom, study, and bath for Jean. On the floor above a room was set apart for Giusippe, so that he might stay at the house whenever he chose. Saturday nights and Sundays he always spent at Uncle Tom's; the rest of the time he lived with his uncle and aunt.

To Giusippe it was good to be once more with his kin and talk in his native language; and yet such a transformation had a few months in the United States made in him that he found that he was less and less anxious to remain an Italian and more and more eager to become an American. His uncle, who had made but a poor success of life in Venice, and who had secured in his foster country prosperity and happiness, declared there was no land like it. He missed, it is true, the warm, rich beauty of his birthplace beyond the seas, and many a time talked of it to his wife and Giusippe; but the lure of the great throbbing American city gripped him with its fascination. It presented endless opportunity—the chance to learn, to possess, to win out.

"If you have brains and use them, if you are not afraid of hard work, there is no limit to what a man may do and become over here," he told Giusippe. "That is why I like it, and why I never shall go back to Italy. Just you jump in, youngster, and don't you worry but you'll bring up somewhere in the end."

There was no need to urge a lad of Giusippe's make-up to "jump in"; on the contrary it might, perhaps, have been wiser advice to caution him not to take his new work too hard. He toiled early and late, never sparing himself, never thinking of fatigue. Physically he was a rugged boy, and to this power was linked the determination to make good. Before he had been a month in the glass house he was recognized by all the men as one who would make of each task merely a stepping-stone to something higher. His uncle was congratulated right and left on having such a nephew, and very proud indeed he was of Giusippe.

In the meantime Uncle Tom Curtis, although apparently busy with more important matters, kept his eyes and ears open. Frequent reports concerning his protégé reached him in his far-away office at the other end of the works. Indeed the boy would have been not a little surprised had he known how very well informed about his progress the head of the firm really was. But Uncle Tom never said much. He did, however, write Uncle Bob that to bring home a penniless Italian as a souvenir of Venice was not such a crazy scheme after all as he had at first supposed it. From Uncle Tom this was rare praise, a complete vindication, in fact. Uncle Bob chuckled over the letter and showed it to Hannah, who rubbed her hands and declared things were working out nicely.

"Some day, Giusippe," remarked Uncle Tom one evening after dinner, when together with the young people he was sitting within the crimson glow of the library lamp, "I propose you take Jean through the works. It is ridiculous that a niece of mine should acquaint herself with the history of the glass of all the past ages and never go through her own uncle's factory. What do you say, missy? Would you like to go?"

"Of course, Uncle Tom, I'd love to. I wrote Uncle Bob only the other day that I wanted dreadfully to see how plate glass was made and hoped some time you'd take me. I didn't like to ask you for fear you were too busy."

"I have been a little rushed, I'll admit. We business men," he slapped Giusippe on the shoulder, "live in a good deal of a whirl—eh, Giusippe?"

"I know you do, sir."

"And you? You have nothing to do, I suppose. It chances that I have heard to the contrary, my lad. You've put in some mighty good work since you came here, and I am much gratified by the spirit you've shown."

Giusippe glowed. It was not a common thing for Mr. Curtis to commend.

"I didn't know, sir, that you——"

"Knew what you were doing? Didn't any one ever tell you that I have a search-light and a telescope in my office?" Uncle Tom laughed. "Oh, I keep track of things even if I do seem to be otherwise occupied. So look out for yourself! Beware! My eyes may be upon you almost any time."

"I am not afraid, sir," smiled the boy.

"And you have no cause to be, either, my lad," was Uncle Tom's serious rejoinder. "Now you and Jean fix up some date to see the works. Why not to-morrow? It is Saturday, and she will not be at school."

"But I work Saturday mornings, Mr. Curtis."

"Can't somebody else do your work for you?"

"I have never asked that."

"Well, I will. We'll arrange it. Let us say to-morrow then. Take Jean and explain things to her. You can do it, can't you?"

"I think so. Most of the process I understand now, and if there is anything that I need help about I can ask."

"That's right. Just go ahead and complete the girl's education in glass-making so she can write her Boston uncle that she is now qualified to superintend any glass works that may require her oversight."

Jean laughed merrily.

"I am afraid I should be rather a poor superintendent, Uncle Tom," said she. "There seems to be such a lot to know about glass."

"There is," agreed Mr. Curtis. "Sometimes I feel as if about everything in the world was made of it. Of course you've seen the ink erasers made of a cluster of fine glass fibres. Oh, yes; they have them. And the aigrettes made in the same way and used in ladies' bonnets. Then there are those beautiful brocades having fine threads of spun glass woven into them in place of gold and silver; it was a Toledo firm, by the way, that presented to the Infanta Eulalie of Spain a dress of satin and glass woven together. To-day came an order from California for glass to serve yet another purpose; you could never guess what. The people out there want some of our heaviest polished plate to make the bottoms of boats."

"Of boats!"

"Boats," repeated Uncle Tom, nodding.

"But—but why make a glass-bottomed boat?"

"Well, in California, Florida, and many other warm climates boats with bottoms of glass are much in use. Sightseers go out to where the water is clear and by looking down through the transparent bottom of the boat they can see, as they go along, the wonderful plant and animal life of the ocean. Such reptiles, such fish, such seaweeds as there are! I have heard that it is as interesting as moving pictures, and quite as thrilling, too."

"I'd like to do it," said Giusippe.

"I shouldn't," declared Jean with a shudder. "I hate things

that writhe, and squirm, and wriggle. Imagine being so near those hideous creatures! Why, if I once should see them I should never dare to go in bathing again. I'd rather not know what's in the sea."

"There is something in that, little lady," Uncle Tom answered, slipping one of his big hands over the two tiny ones in the girl's lap. "Giusippe and I will keep the sea monsters out of your path, then; and the land monsters, too, if we can. Now it is time you children got to bed, for to-morrow you must make an early start. You'd better telephone your aunt or uncle that you are going to stay here to-night, Giusippe. If you do not work to-morrow you will not need to get to the factory until Jean and I do; it will be much simpler for you to remain here and go down with us in the car. I'll call up your boss and explain matters. Good-night, both of you. Now scamper! I want to read my paper."

The next morning the Curtis family was promptly astir, and after breakfast Uncle Tom with his two charges rolled off to the factory in the big red limousine.

"Your superintendent says you are welcome to the morning off, Giusippe," Mr. Curtis remarked as they sped along. "But he did have the grace to say he should miss you. Now it seems to me that if you are to give Jean a clear idea of what we do at the works you better begin with the sheet glass department. That will interest her, I am sure; later you can show her where you yourself work."

The car pulled up at Mr. Curtis's office, and they all got out.

"Good-bye! Good luck to you," he called as the boy and girl started off.

Jean waved her hand.

"We will be back here and ready to go home with you, Uncle Tom, at one o'clock," she called over her shoulder.

"We won't be late, sir."

"See that you're not. I shall be hungry and shall not want to wait. I guess you'll have an appetite, too, by that time."

"Is sheet glass blown, Giusippe?" inquired Jean, as they went across the yard. "I hate to ask stupid questions, but you see I do not know anything about it."

"That isn't a stupid question. Quite the contrary. Yes, sheet glass is blown. You shall see it done, too."

"But I do not understand how they can get it flattened out, if they blow it."

"You will."

The boy led the way through a low arched door.

Before the furnaces within the great room a number of glass-blowers were at work. They stood upon wooden stagings, each one of which was built over a well or pit in the floor, and was just opposite an opening in the furnace.

"Each of these men has a work-hole of the furnace to himself, so that he may heat his material any time he needs to do so. The staging gives him room to swing his heavy mass of glass as he blows it, and the pit in the floor, which is about ten feet deep, furnishes space for the big cylinder to run out, or grow longer, as he blows. The gathering for sheet glass is done much as was that for the smaller pieces. The gatherer collects a lump on his pipe, cools it a little, and collects more until he has enough. He then rests it on one of those wooden blocks such as you see over there; the block is hollowed out so to let the blower expand the glass to the diameter he wants it."

"But I should think the block would burn when the hot glass is forced inside it."

"It would if it were not first sprinkled with water. Sometimes hollow metal blocks are used instead. In that case water passes through to keep them cool, and they are dusted over with charcoal to keep them from sticking, and from scratching the glass. After a sufficiently large mass of glass has been gathered and reheated to a workable condition the blower begins his task. First he swings the great red-hot lump about so that it will get longer. His aim is to make a long cylinder and into it he must blow constantly in order to keep it full of air. Watch that man now at work. See how deft he is, and how strong. The even thickness of the glass, and the uniformity of its size, depend entirely upon his skill. If he finds the cylinder running out too fast, or in other words getting too long, he shifts it up over his head, always taking care, however, to keep it upright."

Jean watched.

How rapidly the man worked with the great mass on his blow-pipe! Now he blew it far down into the pit beneath, where it hung like a mighty, elongated soap-bubble; now he swung it to and fro; now lifted it above his head. And all the time he was blowing into it blasts of air from his powerful lungs.

"The cylinder doesn't seem to get any bigger round," observed Jean at last.

"No. Its diameter was fixed at the beginning by the wooden block. That settles its size once and for all; it is the length and thickness of the cylinder which are governed by the blower. Do you realize how strong a man has to be to wield such a weight as that lump of metal? It is no easy matter. Luckily he can suspend it against that wooden rest if he gets too tired. In England they use a sort of iron frame called an *Iron Man* to relieve the blower of the weight of the glass and the device was also used at one time in Belgium; but the Belgian workmen gradually did away with it."

For a long time the two children stood there fascinated by the skill of the blowers.

"Suppose we go on now and see the rest of the process," suggested Giusippe, a little unwillingly. "I could watch these men all day, but we have much to do, and if we do not hurry we shall not get through."

The next step in the work was opening out the cylinders, and this was done in two ways. The end of those made of thinner glass was put into the furnace while at the same time air was forced inside through the blow-pipe. As a result the air expanded by the heat of the fire, and burst open the cylinder at its hottest or weakest end. By placing this opening downward it was widened to the diameter necessary. The cylinders of thicker glass were opened by fastening to one end a lump of hot metal, thereby weakening them at this point. When the air was forced in by the blower it burst open the mass and the break thus made was enlarged by cutting it round with the scissors.

"Now come on, Jean, and see them flatten it out," said Giusippe.

Upon a wooden rest or chevalet the cylinder was now laid and detached from the pipe by placing a bit of cold steel against the part of the glass that still clung to the blow-pipe. At once the neck of the glass, which was hot, contracted at the touch of the cold metal and broke away from the pipe. The small end was then taken off by winding round it a thread of hot glass, and afterward applying cold iron or steel at any point the thread had covered.

"The cylinder is now finished at top and bottom and is ready to be split up the side," said Giusippe. "This they do with a rule and a diamond point mounted in a long handle. The diamond point is drawn along the inside of the cylinder and opens it out flat. If there are any imperfections in the glass the cutter plans to have them come as near the edge of this opening as possible so there will be little waste."

Jean nodded.

"Now, as you will see, the glass is ready for the flattener. First he warms it in the flue of his furnace and then, using his croppie or iron, he puts it on the flattening-stone; if you look carefully you will see that the top of this stone is covered with a large sheet of glass. In the heat of the furnace the cylinder with the split uppermost soon opens out and falls back in a wavy mass. See?"

Jean watched intently as the great roll of glass unfolded and spread into billows. The moment it was fairly open the flattener took his polissoir, a rod of iron with a block of wood at one end, and began smoothing out the uneven sheet of glass into a flat surface. At times he had to rub it with all his strength to straighten it. This done the flattening-stone was moved on wheels to a cooler part of the furnace and the sheet of glass upon it was transferred to a cooling-stone. When stiff enough it was taken off and placed either flat or on edge in a rack with other sheets.

So the process went on.

Cylinder after cylinder was blown, opened up, flattened, and annealed. So quickly did the single sheets of glass cool that it was not much more than half an hour from the time they entered the flattening kiln before they came out thoroughly annealed. They were then carried to the warehouse for inspection and the especially fine ones were selected to be polished into patent glass. The sheets were rated as bests, seconds, thirds, and fourths, and their average size was 48 x 34 or 36 inches, although the foreman said that sometimes sheets as large as 82 x 42 or 75 x 50 had been made. These, however, were exceedingly difficult to handle, as they were in constant danger of being broken. The mass of glass was also very heavy for the blower to wield.

"The great advantage of sheet glass over crown glass is that it can be made in large pieces. Of course it is not as brilliant as crown, but it is much more useful," added the workman.

"What is crown glass?" whispered Jean to Giusippe.

"It is a variety of glass manufactured by another process," was the reply. "We do not make it here. Do you remember the bull's eye glass windows we saw in England? Well, each of those bull's eyes came from the center of a sheet of crown glass just where a lump of hot glass was attached so the blower could whirl or spin it from the middle and make it into a flat disc. But, as you can readily understand, a sheet of glass with this mark or defect right in the center will never cut to advantage, and therefore only comparatively small pieces can be got out of it; there is much waste. Yet, as the man says, it has a wonderfully brilliant surface. Now I am not going to let you stay here any longer or we shall not have time to see the part of the factory where I am working. I'm in the plate

"THE MELT IS POURED OUT ON AN IRON TABLE"

glass department, and I intend to drag you off to the casting hall this very moment."

Jean laughed.

"Before you go, though, you must understand that plate glass is quite a different thing from these others. It is not blown at all. Instead the melt is poured out on an iron table just as molasses candy is turned out of a pan to cool. You'll see how it is done."

They crossed the yard and entered another part of the works; Giusippe gave the foreman a word of greeting as they went in.

On each side of the great room were the annealing ovens, and down the center of the hall on a track moved a casting table which rolled along on wheels. The pots of molten glass or metal were first taken from the furnaces and carried on trucks to this casting table. Here they were lifted by a crane, suspended above the table, and then tilted over, and the glass poured out.

"For all the world like a pan of fudge!" declared Jean.

Giusippe laughed.

"I guess you would find it the stickiest, heaviest fudge you ever tried to manage," said he.

The instant the mass of soft metal was on the table a roller of cast-iron was passed very swiftly back and forth over it, spreading it to uniform thickness, and at the same time flattening it.

"The thickness of the glass is gauged by the strips of iron on which the roller moves," explained Giusippe to Jean. "These can be adjusted to any thickness. Notice how rapidly the men have to work. The glass must be finished while it is hot, or there will be flaws in it. It is a rushing job, I can tell you."

"But—but you don't call this stuff plate glass, do you?" inquired the girl in dismay. "It does not look like it—at least not like any I ever saw used as shop windows or for mirrors."

"Oh, it is not done yet. But it is what we call rough plate. That's the kind that is used where light and not transparency is needed. You often see it in office doors or in skylights of buildings. To get the beautiful polished plate glass that you are talking about this rough plate must be polished over and over again. But before it can be polished it must first be annealed as rough plate. It goes into the annealing ovens right from this table and comes out all irregular—full of pits and imperfections. No matter how flat the casting table is, or how much care is taken, the surface of the glass after annealing is always bad. If it is to be made into polished plate it must be ground down first with sand and water; then ground smoother still with a coarse kind of emery stone and water; next ground again with water and powdered emery stone. After that comes the smoothing process done with a finer sort of emery and water. Last of all the sheet is bedded, as we call it, and each side is polished with rouge, or red oxide, between moving pads of felt."

"Goodness!" ejaculated Jean. "Do you mean to say they have to go through all that with every sheet of plate glass?"

"Every sheet of *polished* plate," corrected Giusippe. "Rough plate does not need to be polished or ground down much. It is made merely for use and not for beauty. Sometimes to add strength, and help support the weight of large sheets, wire netting is embedded in them. Wired glass like this was the invention of an American named Schuman and it is used a great deal; the wire not only relieves the weight of the glass but serves the double purpose of holding the pieces should any break off and start to fall. Often, too, insurance companies specify that it shall be used as a matter of fire protection."

"But I should think if plate glass—I mean polished plate," Jean hurriedly corrected her error, "has to be ground down so much there wouldn't be anything left of it. It must come out dreadfully thin."

"The casters have to consider that and allow for it," answered the Italian. "They expect part of the glass will have to be ground away, so they cast it thicker in the first place. A large, perfect sheet of polished plate is quite an achievement. From beginning to end it requires the greatest care, and if spoiled it is a big loss not only in actual labor but because of the amount of material required to make it. Even at the very last it may be injured in the warehouse either by scratching or breaking. It is there that it is cut in the size pieces desired."

"How?"

"With a rule and diamond point just such as is used for cutting sheet glass. The surface is scratched to give the line of fracture and then it is split evenly."

"I should hate to have the responsibility of cutting or handling it when it is all done," Jean observed with a little shiver.

"Well you might. Only men of the greatest skill and experience are allowed to touch the big, heavy sheets. The risk is too great. They turn only the best workmen into the plate glass department."

"But you work here, don't you, Giusippe?"

"I? Oh, I—I'm just learning," was the boy's modest reply.

"You seem to have learned pretty well," said a voice at his elbow.

Turning the lad was astonished to find Mr. Curtis standing just behind him.

"I must own up to being an eavesdropper," laughed the older man. "I couldn't resist knowing whether you were instructing Jean as she should be instructed, Giusippe. Don't worry. I have no fault to find. I couldn't have explained it better myself. You shall have your diploma on plate glass making any time you want it."

Then as the superintendent advanced to speak to him, Mr. Curtis added:

"You had given your pupil a good bringing up, Mr. Hines. He does you credit."

CHAPTER XI

JEAN'S TELEGRAM AND WHAT IT SAID

HE winter in Pittsburgh passed rapidly. For Jean it was a happy year despite much hard work at school, German lessons with Fräulein, and long hours of piano practising. It seemed as if the scales and finger exercises were endless and sometimes the girl wondered which had the more miserable fate—she who was forced to drum the same old things over and over, or poor Uncle Tom who had to listen when she was doing it. And yet as she looked back over her busy days she realized that she neither studied nor practised all the time. No, there was many a good time interspersed in her routine. For example, there was the Shakespeare play at the school, a performance of "As You Like It," in which Jean herself took the part of "Rosalind." This was an excitement indeed! Uncle Tom became so interested that he got out his book and spent several evenings coaching the leading lady, as he called the girl; one night he even went so far as to

130

impersonate "Orlando," and he and Jean gave a dress rehearsal in the library, greatly to Giusippe's delight and amusement. This set them all to reading Shakespeare aloud, and going to a number of presentations of the dramas then being given in the city. To the young people all this was new and wonderful, for up to the present they had been little to the theater.

In the meantime Giusippe was also having his struggles. It was a rushing season at the factory, there being many large orders to fill; the mill hummed night and day and in consequence the scores of glass-makers looked happy and prosperous. No one was out of employment or on half pay, and none of the workmen dreaded Christmas because there was nothing to put in the kiddies' stockings.

With Christmas came Uncle Bob and oh, what a holiday there was then! Was ever a Christmas tree so beautiful, or a Christmas dinner so delicious? Giusippe brought his aunt and uncle to the great house, and in the evening there was a dance for Jean and some of her school friends. Uncle Bob, who was in the gayest of spirits, danced with all the girls; introduced everybody to everybody; and brought heaping plates of salad to the dancers. There seemed to be nothing he could not do from putting up Christmas greens to play-ing the piano until the belated musicians arrived. The party could never had been given without him, that was certain. It was a Christmas long to be remembered!

And when he left the next morning it was with the under-standing that Jean should return to Boston the first of May. Uncle Tom looked pretty grave when he was reminded that the days of his niece's stay with him were numbered; and it was amusing to hear him use the very arguments that Uncle

Bob had voiced when Jean had left Boston for Pittsburgh months before.

"It isn't as if the child was never coming back," he told Giusippe. "Her home is here; she is only going to Boston for her vacation. We should be selfish indeed to grudge her a few weeks at the seashore. Pittsburgh is rather warm in summer."

Thus Uncle Tom consoled himself, and as the days flew past tried to put out of his mind the inevitable day of parting.

Then came May and with it a very unexpected happening. Jean's trunk was packed, and she was all ready to leave for the East, when Uncle Tom was taken sick.

"I doubt if it is anything but overwork and fatigue," said the doctor. "Mr. Curtis has, I find, been carrying a great deal of care this winter. It is good to do a rushing business, of course, but when one has to rush along with it the wear and tear on the nerves is pretty severe."

"You don't think he will be ill long, do you?" questioned Jean anxiously.

"I cannot tell. Such cases are uncertain. He just needs rest—to give up work for a while and stay at home. Recreation, diversion, amusement—that's what he wants. Read to him; motor with him; walk with him; keep him entertained. Things like that will do far more good than medicine."

"But—but—I'm—I'm going away to-morrow for the rest of the summer," stammered Jean.

"Away? Humph! That's unfortunate."

"Why, you don't really think I am any use here, do you? Enough use to remain, I mean," the girl inquired in surprise. "Uncle Tom doesn't—you don't mean that he *needs* me; that I could do good by staying?"

A flush overspread her face. That any one should need her! And most of all such a big strong man as Uncle Tom. The idea was unbelievable. Hitherto life had been a matter of what others should do for her. She had been a child with no obligations save to do as she was told. Her two uncles whom she loved so much had discussed her fate and decided between them what her course should be. Now, all at once, there was no pilot at the wheel. The directing of the ship fell to her guidance. In the space of those few moments, as if by a miracle, Jean Cabot ceased to be a child and became a woman.

"Mr. Curtis is very fond of you, isn't he?" asked the physician. "He will miss you if you are not here, I am afraid. Who else is there in the house to be a companion for him?"

"No one but Fräulein, and of course she is getting older and is not very strong."

"Unfortunate!" repeated the doctor.

"It is not at all necessary for me to go to-morrow," Jean said quickly. "I can postpone it and stay here just as well as not, and I think it would be much better if I did." She spoke with deepening conviction. "I'll telegraph my uncle in Boston and explain to him that I cannot leave just now."

What a deal of dignity stole into that single word "cannot."

At last there was a duty to fulfil toward some one else— some one who really needed her. Jean repeated the amazing fact over and over to herself. She had a place to fill. She and Uncle Tom had reversed their obligations; he was now the weak one, she the strong.

With a happy heart the girl went back up-stairs.

Uncle Tom was lying very still in bed, his face turned away from the door; but he heard her light step and put out his hand.

"My little girl," he whispered.

Jean slipped her soft palm into his.

"Did I wake you?"

"No, dear. I was not asleep. I cannot sleep these days. Last night I heard the clock strike almost every hour. It has been so right along. I cannot recall when I have had a full night's rest. No sooner do I go to bed than my mind travels like a whirlwind over everything I've done through the day. There is no peace, no stopping it."

"We will stop it, dear. Don't worry, Uncle Tom. The doctor says you are just a little tired, and he is going to give you some medicine that will help you to feel better. Then you are to stay at home and rest for a while. To-morrow you shall have your breakfast in bed and later, when it is sunny and warm, I shall take you for a nice motor ride."

"But—but you forget, girlie, that to-morrow you won't be here."

"Oh, yes I shall. I'm going to stay. There is no law against my changing my mind and not going to Boston, is there?"

Jean smiled down at him.

"I've wired Uncle Bob that I am going to postpone my visit," she added.

A light came into the man's eyes.

"Did the doctor——?"

"No, he didn't. I decided it myself. Do you suppose for a moment I'd leave you just when you are going to be here at home and have some time to entertain me? Indeed, no! Lately you've been so busy that you couldn't take me anywhere. Now you are to desert the office and be under my orders for a while. Oh, we'll do lots of nice things. We'll go off in the motor and see all sorts of places I've wanted to see; and we'll walk; and we'll read some of those books we have been trying to get time to read together. We shall have great fun."

Mr. Curtis looked keenly at the girl for a few seconds.

"Perhaps," he remarked at last, "it won't make much difference to Uncle Bob if you do postpone your visit for a week or two."

"I am sure it won't."

There was a deep sigh of satisfaction from the invalid.

"I'm glad you've decided to stay, little girl. Somehow it would be about the last straw to have you leave now. I'd miss you in any case, of course; but if I have got to be home here and round the house it does not seem as if I could stand it to have you gone."

"I wouldn't think of going and leaving you, dear. Put your mind at rest. I intend to stay right here until you are quite well again."

She bent down and gently kissed her uncle's forehead.

It seemed as if that kiss smoothed every wrinkle of worry from the man's brow.

Quietly Jean tiptoed across the room and drew down the shade; then she dropped into a chair beside the bed and took up a book. For some time she sat very still, her eyes intent upon the page. Then at last she glanced up. Uncle Tom's head had fallen back on the pillows and for the first time in many days he slept.

So did Jean Cabot find her summer planned for her. Instead of joining Uncle Bob and enjoying months of bathing and sailing on the North Shore she helped nurse Uncle Tom Curtis back to health. For the breakdown proved to be of much longer duration than any of them had foreseen. The exhausted system was slow in reacting and it was weeks before the turning point toward recovery was reached. During those tedious hours of waiting Jean was the sole person who could bring a smile to the sick man's face or rouse in him a shadow of interest in what was going on about him. "Her price was above rubies," the doctor said. She was better than sunshine or fresh air; she was, in fact, the only hope of bringing the invalid back to his normal self.

And when those grim days passed and Uncle Tom began to be better, how he clung to the girl—clung to her with an affection which neither of them had felt before. It was the realization of his dependence that made Jean send to Uncle Bob that letter, the last lines of which read:

"I feel more strongly than I can tell you, dear Uncle Bob, that for the present my place is here. Uncle Tom needs me and cannot do without me. You have Hannah to help you keep house and you can get on; but he has nobody but me. When he is quite strong again I will come to Boston, but until I do I am sure you'll understand that although I cannot be with you, I love you just the same.

"Jean."

A reply came back by wire.

"Goodness!" exclaimed Jean as she opened the long telegram. "I hope nothing is the matter. Uncle Bob never sends telegrams. He must have been reckless to spend his money on such a long message as this."

"You are doing just right. Stay as long as needed, but remember Boston home waits whenever you wish to come. Hannah has proved inadequate housekeeper. Have new one. Miss Cartright and I were married in New York to-day.

"Uncle Bob."

Jean's reading stopped with a jerk. She was speechless. So great was her joy, her surprise, that not a word would come to her tongue.

Then Uncle Tom remarked dryly:

"I guess your Uncle Bob was a bit reckless about the time he sent that wire. The only wonder is the telegram wasn't twice as long."

Giusippe was the next to find his voice.

"Well!" he ejaculated. "And we never even dreamed it! At last, Jean, you've got your wish. Your good fairy has given you an *aunt*!"

"And such an aunt!" Jean added.

CHAPTER XII

JEAN AND GIUSIPPE EACH FIND A NICHE IN LIFE

URING Uncle Tom's illness and slow recovery Giusippe became the messenger between Mr. Curtis's residence and his office. It was, however, weeks before there was any link connecting the two. But as health returned there came to the invalid a gradual revival of interest in affairs at the glass works. Nevertheless the doctor was a cautious man and at first permitted only the slightest allusions to be made to business. Later, as strength increased, Mr. Curtis was allowed to look over at home mail, papers, and specifications and put his signature to a few important documents, and since Giusippe was almost constantly at the house what was more natural than that he should become the go-between? Mr. Curtis dropped into explaining to the boy from time to time many confidential matters and directing him as to what he wished done regarding them. The young Italian, as his employer soon found, was quick to grasp a situation and

138

could be relied upon to fulfil instructions to the letter and without blundering. Such a person was of inestimable value during those days of convalescence.

So it came about that Giusippe spent less and less of his time in his own department in the glass works and more and more in Mr. Curtis's private office. Before long, boy though he was, he had quite a complete comprehension of the older man's affairs and proved himself most useful to the head of the firm who was fighting his way back to health. It was so easy to say:

"Regarding this letter, I wish, Giusippe, you would see that such and such a reply is sent. Look it over yourself before it goes out to be sure that the stenographer has correctly caught my idea."

Or:

"Go and tell Levin of the sheet glass department that I want these orders filled before any others are shipped. Attend to it yourself, and make certain he clearly understands."

To drop any portion of the detail of his mighty business upon younger shoulders, or in fact upon any shoulders at all was a thing which, but a short time before, Mr. Curtis would have considered impossible. But now, to his surprise, he found himself actually doing it to an amazing extent, and discovered that no calamity resulted in consequence. On the contrary it was a positive relief to have a bright, strong, eager boy lift a part of the burden which had become so heavy for the older man to bear alone. For Giusippe possessed that rare gift seldom found in the young and often lacking, even, in elder persons—he could hold his tongue. He never prattled of Mr. Curtis's affairs; never boasted of his knowledge of the

"I WANT THESE ORDERS FILLED"

innermost workings of the firm. He did as he was told, gave his opinion when asked, and kept whatever information was doled out to him entirely to himself.

Hence it followed naturally that when Uncle Tom began going to the works for a few hours each day he took Giusippe with him, and when he came home left the boy to see carried out the instructions he gave. Slowly the office force began to defer to the youthful Italian.

"Did Mr. Curtis say anything about this matter or that?"

"Was such and such a price the one Mr. Curtis wished quoted?"

Having discussed many of these very matters with his employer Giusippe was usually ready with an answer or he could get one. For it was he alone who was sure to receive a telephone reply from the Curtis residence; he was the only one who knew at just what time of day Mr. Curtis could be reached, and whether he was well enough that morning to be disturbed. Men desiring interviews with the head of the firm soon found themselves inquiring for Mr. Cicone and asking him if possible to arrange things so they could have a few words with Mr. Curtis. Giusippe was the recognized buffer, the go-between who guarded the capitalist from annoyance and intrusion of every sort.

"You talk with this fellow, Giusippe," Mr. Curtis would often say. "Tell him—well, you know—get him out of the office. You can do it politely. Tell him I'll give him a hundred dollars toward his hospital, but keep him out of my way."

Then Giusippe would laugh.

He had begun to understand that the life of a rich man was no easy one.

Scores of persons came to see Mr. Curtis: persons applying for business positions; persons begging money for various good causes; customers; salesmen; men wanting newspaper interviews. From morning until night the throng filed in and out of the office. Up to the present Mr. Curtis had been content to remain in the security of his inner domain and rely on his stenographer to fill many of the gaps. But with illness a change had come and it was to Giusippe that most of these duties fell.

And yet, strangely enough, nothing had been further from the older man's original plan than to transform this foreign-born lad into his private secretary. But so it came about.

"I seem to just need you all the time, Giusippe," he declared one day. "When you leave the house and return to your uncle's I am always discovering something I meant to ask you and having to send the car after you; and the moment you go back to your own job in the casting department, without fail some matter comes up and you have to be telephoned for. It is no use to try to get on without you. I need you all the time. I need you here at home and I need you at the office."

Giusippe smiled.

"I'm glad if I can be of help to you, sir."

"You are of help; you are more than that—you are——See here, what do you say to throwing up your position at the works and coming into my private office as my—well, as my general utility man? I've never had a secretary—I've never wanted one; and if I had I never before have seen the chap I'd trust with the job. But you are different. You're one of the family, to begin with. Moreover, you've proved that you can be trusted, and that you have some common sense.

What would you take to move into your room up-stairs for good and all, and live here where I can get hold of you when I want you? Are you so wedded to your aunt and uncle or to your work in the factory that you would be unwilling to make the change?"

A flush suffused the boy's face.

"If you really think that I could do for you what you want done, Mr. Curtis——"

"I don't think, I know!"

"Then I'd like to come, sir."

"That's right! It will be a weight off my mind. The doctor says that for some months I must still go easy. You can save both my time and my strength. I like you and I believe you like me; that is half the battle in working with any one. We will send to your uncle's for your trunk and whatever else you have."

"There isn't much else but some books," answered Giusippe. "I have been buying a few from time to time as I could afford them."

"Box them up and send them over. Send everything. This is to be your future home, you understand. And by the by, we'll give you that other room adjoining your bedroom. You will need a bit more space. I will have a desk and some book-shelves put in there."

"Thank you, sir."

"We'll call that settled, then. It is going to be very helpful to have you right here on the spot. It is the person who aims to be of service who is really valuable in the world. Look at Jean. In her way she has been doing the same thing that you have. When she found I was in a hole and needed her she gave up her vacation in the East without a murmur. I sha'n't forget it, either. Come in, missy. I'm talking about you."

Jean, who had paused on the threshold of the room, entered smiling.

"You caught me at just the right moment, little lady. I was slandering you," went on Mr. Curtis. "I was saying to Giusippe that I never again can get on without you two young persons. Why, this old house was quiet as the grave before you came into it. I cannot imagine how I ever existed here alone all these years. The piano wasn't opened from one end of the year to the other, and when I unlocked the door and came in there wasn't a single sound anywhere. As I look back on it I guess I spent about all my time at the Club. But since you came it has been different. I've liked it a whole lot better, too. Now I feel as if I really had a home."

Jean bent down and kissed him.

"When I get older," she said, "I mean that you shall have even a nicer home. Fräulein will be an old lady soon, Uncle Tom, and will not be able to take care of things as she does now. Then I'm going to ask her to teach me to market and to keep house. If you are to make Giusippe your secretary it is only fair that you should give me a position, too. I'll be your housekeeper. You'll see what a good one I shall make after I've learned how. I should love to do it. A girl—a really, truly girl, Uncle Tom, can't help wanting to keep house for somebody."

"No more she can, dear, and she ought to want to, too. It is her work in the world to be a homemaker—the one who touches with comfort and with beauty the lives of those about her. You shall be housekeeper for Giusippe and me, little girl, and shall make out of these four walls a real home. That is what your new Aunt Ethel is to do for your Uncle Bob."

"I know it," answered Jean softly. "Even Uncle Bob couldn't get on without some one to look after him, could he?"

"No," answered Mr. Curtis, "and it is fortunate he has found some one if you are to be my housekeeper. If he makes any trouble we'll just remind him that it was only your summers that you were to spend with him. Your winters belong to me."

"I don't believe he will quarrel about it," was Jean's answer. "He won't need me now, and he will understand that you do."

"I sure do," replied Uncle Tom, drawing the girl to his side. "I need both of you—my boy and my girl."

9 781761 534669